## THE RANTH HAVEN'T FORGOTTEN HOW TO FIGHT

Krral crept to the door and peered in. There were two of them, both carrying weapons—burners, compact laser pistols. Moving very gently, Krral opened one of the pouches on his harness. From it he took two long, pointed metal spikes. With a sudden, fluid movement, he stepped into the room and flung one of the spikes. There was a gasp of pain, a shower of gore and fur.

Krral rolled. But the hiss of the burner was only inches behind . . .

BOOK THREE OF
*THE QUESTIONER TRILOGY*

# DARK PARADISE

## DENNIS SCHMIDT

ACE BOOKS, NEW YORK

This book is an Ace original edition,
and has never been previously published.

DARK PARADISE

An Ace Book / published by arrangement with
the author

PRINTING HISTORY
Ace edition / November 1990

ISBN: 0-441-69780-1

Ace Books are published by The Berkley Publishing Group,
200 Madison Avenue, New York, NY 10016.
The name "ACE" and the "A" logo
are trademarks belonging to Charter Communications, Inc.

PRINTED IN THE UNITED STATES OF AMERICA

10  9  8  7  6  5  4  3  2  1

*This book is dedicated to Kristina*

# PROLOGUE

*Every questioning is a seeking.*
*Every seeking takes its direction beforehand*
*from what is sought.*

Martin Heidegger
Being and Time

꧁꧂

The creature came from the left, teeth flashing, claws slashing. Seeker moved ever so slightly to the right, pivoted on its right leg, and bent its upper body backward. The attacker's teeth snapped on empty air and its claws barely touched the Questioner's honey-colored fur.

Landing deftly on all fours, the beast spun about to attack again. It leapt, a furious froth spraying from its gaping mouth, its eyes glowing red with a killing rage. Once more Seeker adroitly sidestepped, avoiding the attack rather than meeting it. The way H*mb*l would, the Questioner thought. H*mb*l never kills anything. Instead, the hummer dances with it, becoming one with it, merging and flowing with it, until it can no longer tell the dancer from itself and simply stops its attack.

Seeker dodged again, a slight smile curving its mouth. Sharp teeth barely showed. I, on the other hand, it mused, can only dance this dance of avoidance and hope that sooner or later my attacker will simply give up in exhaustion or disgust. Teeth, mad eyes, and reaching claws flew at Seeker yet again. As it twisted out of the way once more, the Questioner judged that this one would wear out before it quit. And that would take some time. Seeker sighed. I'd rather not kill it, nasty as it is. It's only protecting its cubs. And when I was a Nurturer I would have acted just as ferociously to save my cubs from danger. Besides, it's as much part of Labyrinth as I am and just as worthy of living. So . . .

It took ten or twelve more assaults before the beast stopped and stared with frustrated bewilderment at the Questioner. Its tongue was lolling out, its chest heaving, and its legs sagging from weariness. With a weak snarl, it gathered itself for one last try. But even the effort of trying took more energy than it had left. With a moan, it crumpled heavily to the ground about a foot from Seeker. Seeker, a broad smile on its face, reached out gingerly and touched the creature gently on the head. "Sleep soundly, little one. Your cubs are safe from me. You did your job well. You would have made a good Nurturer."

The Questioner straightened up and looked around. The sun was nearing the horizon in the west. In no more than two hours twilight would fall and then night. Even for a Questioner, night was no time to be out on the surface of Labyrinth. The planet was deadly enough in daytime. At night it was even more lethal. Time to head back to Start, Seeker decided.

It paused for a moment before starting out. Yes, time to be heading back. And time to be heading out as well, it suddenly realized. Back out into the universe and the impossibly dangerous task of being a Questioner. I've been here long enough, resting and recuperating from my last mission. It's time to be going again. It looked around once more, then nodded firmly. Yes, time to be going.

*Seeker.* The Questioner started at the call and gazed around looking for its source. It took a moment to realize the voice was speaking in its own mind. "Ah," it replied. "Longarm?"

*Who else?* came the immediate, sardonic reply. *If you're quite through harassing small, harmless carnivores, I'd appreciate it if you waddled on back to Start.*

Seeker chuckled. "Miss my sparkling presence, eh?"

*Hardly,* Longarm replied drily. *But company's coming and I thought you might like to be here to greet it with me.*

The Questioner blinked in surprise. "Company? Here on Labyrinth? Anybody I know?"

*One,* the Teacher responded grimly. *Bilrog. Or at least what's left of our Furmorian friend. The others you've never met, though I imagine you've heard of them. They're from the planet Ranthar.*

Seeker growled softly with awe. "Ranthar? The Paradise

Planet? What in the name of all my eggs are they doing here? And with Bilrog?''

*That*, Longarm said, *is precisely what I imagine we will find out once they land. Are you coming?*

"On my way," the Questioner answered. It turned in the direction of Start and broke into a lumbering run.

The two of them stood in the gathering twilight and watched the sleek craft slowly settle onto the badly maintained surface of the landing pad. Ranthar, Seeker thought, wonder world of the galaxy. Known throughout the Federation as the Paradise Planet. Tropical by nature, Ranthar had a minimal axial tilt which assured that the difference between seasons was small. Not satisfied with a merely wonderful climate, the Ranth had built a weather control system that guaranteed that each and every day would be perfect.

Ranthar was incredibly rich in resources. Its soils were some of the most fertile in the galaxy and the variety, quantity, and quality of foods that could be grown there were unmatched by any world Seeker had ever heard of. As if the wealth of the home planet were not enough, the Ranth had colonized seven nearby worlds, any one of which was rich enough to stir the envy of the rest of the Federation. Not one of their climates was even remotely comparable to that of the mother world, so the Ranth were busy with the vast task of terraforming every one of them to make them copies of Ranthar.

The Ranth themselves were almost equally as impressive. Bisexual felinoids, they stood upright and reached an average height of six and a half feet. They were superbly muscled with especially powerful chests and arms which ended in six blunt fingers, each tipped with a retractable claw. The Ranth were covered with short, dense fur in a variety of shades, ranging from almost silver to midnight black and an interesting stripe-like pattern that was especially prized. Swift and fierce, they had fought the forces of the last Emperor to a standstill. Warrior to warrior, even the fearsome Furmorians were no better than their equals.

But brawn was only part of the Ranth story. Their science and technology were the envy of the whole galaxy. It was rumored their medical arts were so perfected that they had eradicated disease, virtually reversed the effects of aging, and were well on the way to discovering the secret to immortality. Ranth were said to live at least three hundred years, making them the longest lived mammaloids in the Federation—indeed, in the known universe. Between the richness of the planet and the quality of their medicine, no Ranth was ever hungry or sick. And their star ships, Seeker realized as it gazed at the vehicle that had now come gracefully to a rest on the landing pad, were possibly the most beautiful and advanced crafts that traversed the vast emptiness of space. The ship was glinting silver in color. Its form was long and sleek, with softly rounded curves which indicated it was capable of cleanly slicing through any planet's atmosphere. Its streamlined shape also gave it an impression of vast speed and barely restrained power. It was rumored that Ranth ships were not only superior in speed and maneuverability in normal space, but that they had greatly improved on the standard star-drive and had developed one that was almost twice as fast in 'tweenspace.

What in the world were such creatures doing on Labyrinth? Surely they couldn't be looking for help from a Questioner. And why did they have Bilrog? Seeker fretted anxiously as a door opened in the side of the Ranth ship and a ramp lowered smoothly and noiselessly to the ground.

At the top of the ramp two Ranth appeared, a silver tank laden with dials and mounted on wheels between them. Both the Ranth were superb specimens of their species. The one on the right was a male standing almost seven feet tall. Its fur was creamy beige in color with points of black at the tips of its ears and fingers. The other, at least six and a half feet in height, was a female, dark brown with a single black patch in the center of her chest. Neither wore any clothing other than a harnesslike belt that circled the waist and looped over each shoulder. Various implements with unguessable purposes hung from the harnesses. Moving with graceful power, they came down the ramp with the tank rolling silently between them.

The beige male gave the two waiting figures a haughty looking over. It saw a disparate couple. One was a large, honey-colored creature that vaguely resembled a bear. It stood a little over six feet tall and was nearly as wide. On top of a head that was firmly seated on a powerful neck, a red comb rose in greeting. Two large liquid brown eyes were the most prominent feature of a face that also had a short snout tipped with a black nose and a mouth that showed a rich display of sharp, predator's teeth. Long, powerful arms ended in hands with clawless fingers. The barrellike body was set on two stout, sturdy legs.

The second figure that stood waiting on the ground was a sharp contrast to the first. It was short and decidedly simian in appearance. Its long, hairy arms ended in strong, five-fingered hands that rested lightly on the ground in front of it. Short, bandy legs stuck out below the rather rumpled and tattered brown robe it wore. Beneath the robe, its body was covered with a matted, grey fur that looked like it had never been brushed or groomed. The thick lips on its noseless face were fixed in a perpetual grin. Large, soft eyes with a humorous glint deep within them stared back at the visitors. There was no chin to speak of and the large ears seemed capable of moving freely but for the moment were motionless.

For a moment the male Ranth (or Ranthrr, Seeker remembered) looked back and forth between the two as if trying to make a decision. Finally, as they reached ground level, it threw a salute toward Seeker, raising its right paw in the air, claws extended, then retracting the claws and snapping the arm to its side. "We return your Questioner, Teacher," it said with a haughty rumble.

Longarm cleared its throat. "Ummmm, ummmm. My, my, it seems even Ranthrr make mistakes, eh? Well, well, then, you must be Rruml. Or do you prefer Captain Rruml? I, and not my fuzzy ursoid companion, am the Teacher here."

Rruml turned a withering glance on Longarm. "A simian in charge? I had heard this was a strange planet, but . . ." The Ranthrr let the words hang in the twilight air.

Ignoring the insult, Longarm bustled over to the tank. "Bilrog's in there, eh? What happened?"

The second Ranth, (a female, and so a Ranthaa, Seeker reminded itself) tilted her head to one side and smiled slightly. "Ah, Teacher, your Bilrog is more dead than alive, I fear. We have done all we could."

"Yes, yes, I surmised as much when I saw the stasis tank," the Teacher said impatiently, glancing quickly at the myriad dials that covered the tank. "Hmmmm, hmmmmm, life signs minimal, but still there. Massive trauma, both physically and mentally. What in the name of your pride's honor happened to this Questioner, Tryaal?"

"Ah," the dark Ranthaa purred softly, "you know both my name and my favorite oath, and you can read a stasis tank, something many Ranth cannot do." Tryaal gave Rruml a significant look, arching one eyebrow. "Rruml, you owe the Teacher an apology."

Rruml shifted uncomfortably. "It was a natural mistake. I mean, an ursoid and a simian, well . . . All right, my dear, you are correct. I apologize, Teacher."

Longarm puckered its lips and hooted. "Not necessary, Captain. Your lovely mate is more than compensation for your unintended rudeness. After all, you are a Ranthrr!" The Teacher gave a shout of laughter.

Tryaal chuckled openly as Rruml squirmed in embarrassment. "This simian," she said, "knows more than expected. Truly it is a Teacher. And who is the ursoid, then?"

Seeker dipped its head toward Tryaal. "A Questioner named Seeker, nothing more."

The Ranthaa lifted an eyebrow in amusement. "And nothing less. We are pleased to make your acquaintance, aren't we, Rruml?" She threw a quick glance at the Captain, who nodded reluctantly. "May your pride never be without game."

"And may your hunting always be good," Seeker responded with a slight bow.

"Damn carnivores," Longarm grumbled sourly beneath its breath. "If all of this hunter-killer formality is finished, would you kindly tell me about Bilrog?"

Tryaal nodded. "Bilrog came to Ranthar in response to a Call. A female of our species by the name of Mraal was host. In the course of the mission, Mraal was killed and . . ."

"But," Seeker protested, "if the host was killed while Bilrog was still in it, then Bilrog . . ."

"Would die, too," Longarm completed grimly. "Unless the death of the host marked the end of the mission and Bilrog left just before the death took place, knowing the mission was over."

"But how could the death of the host complete the mission?" Seeker asked, its brow furrowed with uncertainty.

Longarm shrugged. "Since I don't know what the mission was, I can't answer that question. Only Bilrog could, and Bilrog"—the Teacher nodded in the direction of the stasis tank—"is in no condition to tell us. Unless our Ranth friends can enlighten us?'' Longarm cocked its head to one side and fixed Tryaal with a questioning glance.

It was Rruml who answered. ''We have no knowledge of the nature or purpose of the Questioner's mission. We were totally unaware a Questioner had even been Called until ordered to bring this one back to you to care for.''

''Hmmmmmm, hmmmmmm, yes,'' Longarm said musingly, staring at Rruml. ''And yet there is one question you must know the answer to. Yes, one you must be able to shed light on.

''You see, my fine Ranth friends, when a Questioner disengages from its host, it is instantly transferred back to its ship and back into its body. The ship just as instantly jumps and leaves the system to, ah, avoid any unpleasantness that might ensue following the completion of the mission. Ummmm, ummmm, just a precaution, you understand.

''Obviously Bilrog disengaged and got back to the jumpship. Otherwise you would not have found our Furmorian in its own body. Just as obviously something destroyed the jumpship before the ship could jump. Hence the presence of one Questioner, more dead than alive, in a stasis tank. Eh, eh?''

Rruml nodded slowly, grudging respect replacing the arrogant glare on its face. ''Perfectly reasoned, Teacher. Indeed, the only reason we knew the jumpship was there was that we picked up the burst of the warhead as it exploded. When we investigated, we discovered the Questioner, in much the same condition it is now, in the ship's escape module.''

Seeker looked sharply at Longarm. ''Escape module? But, Longarm, our jumpships . . .''

The Teacher held up its hand. ''I know, Seeker. I know. You see, Rruml, the problem with that story is that our jumpships do not contain escape modules.''

Rruml's jaw dropped slightly. ''Your ships don't . . . But then where . . . ?''

''Exactly.'' Longarm chuckled at the Ranthrr's confusion. ''Then where did the module come from and how did Bilrog come to be in it? A problem, to be sure. But,'' the Teacher said with a dismissive shrug, ''equally one we cannot solve here and now.''

Turning to Tryaal, the Teacher bowed slightly. ''Our thanks for returning our Questioner, even though it is somewhat the worse for wear. But I believe that was only part, and probably the minor part, of your reason for coming all the way to Labyrinth from Ranthar. Am I right?''

Tryaal nodded slowly. ''Indeed. We merely brought Bilrog because we were coming anyway.''

''And your reason?''

''We wish another Questioner be sent immediately to Ranthar.''

Seeker looked at Longarm in open astonishment. ''Ranthar wants another Questioner? But why would the paradise planet need a Questioner in the first place, much less a second one?''

Longarm pouted out its lips in thought. ''An interesting question. Interesting indeed. Usually the planets that make a Call for the services of a Questioner are anything but paradises.

''But there is an even more interesting question here, Seeker.'' They all looked at the Teacher. ''Yes, much more interesting. The truly interesting question is why the paradise planet that didn't need a Questioner in the first place tried to murder the first one it Called.

''And you, Seeker, will be lucky enough to have a chance to answer that question.'' Longarm gave a shout of laughter. ''And hopefully to come back and tell me the answer!''

# PART ONE

*The Crossroads Where Thought Hesitates*

# I.

❧⟨❧⟩❧

*At the core of all that is beautiful*
*lies something uncanny*
*and these hills, this soft sky, the shapes of these trees,*
*at this very moment*
*lose the illusion of meaning with which we have clothed them,*
*and from that instant forevermore*
*they become more remote than a paradise lost.*

Albert Camus
The Myth of Sisyphus

"Damnit, Urmaal, I don't need any help for this assignment! I don't need it and I don't want it!"

Urmaal looked calmly at the large Ranth male that stood glowering over her. She appeared calm, but even her patience, tested through the raising of five litters of riotous cubs and almost legendary within the Service, was beginning to wear thin. Indeed, she decided, cubs were easier to deal with than this particular Second Hundred Ranthrr. Cubs were merely nonrational, whereas this damn Krral was positively irrational! But she held herself in careful check since Krral, for all his problems, was one of the very best she had.

Krral's fur was the rare and prized tiger-stripe pattern in black and yellowish grey. He stood a good seven feet tall, which was several inches above average for a full grown Ranthrr. He tipped the scale at two fifty and every ounce was solid muscle and bone. Yet because he was so tall and compact, he didn't seem all that muscular. Indeed, he appeared deceptively soft.

Coming from an excellent bloodline, Krral's physical size and strength were somewhat of a throwback to an earlier era when Ranth had been hunters and killers and warriors. His great grandsire had been one of the heroes of the wars with the Emperor. Also named Krral, he was reputed to have personally killed three Furmorians in individual combat. But the Emperor had finally failed and there had been peace in the Federation for many Hundreds now. Warrior types were no longer in genetic vogue. Krral had been a natural child from his mother's first litter. The genetics there had been nothing but passion and chance and none of the cubs had ever been close to the geneticist's test tubes. The result had been an outstanding, if not stylish, litter. Krral's surviving littermate was a sister who was already high within the colonial administration and from all indications would move yet higher. The brother, who had been a slow-moving, incredibly powerful, and calmly thoughtful Ranth, had died about a year ago in a freak accident on Ranth-urrl-Vynnur. Or at least that's how the records read.

And there was something else one had to consider in the case of Krral . . . the recent loss of his mate, Mraal. Second Hundred pairings like those two had were rare indeed. Very much, she mused fondly, like his mother's or mine with Snurrl. The two of them had met on the colony world of Ranth-urrl-Urthar near the end of their First Hundred. They had had a brief and intense relationship, the kind conventional wisdom said burned out as swiftly as it rose. Back on Ranthar for their Second Hundred, they had both signed for the Service and met again. The passion had burst into flames anew and they had paired without bothering about any of the formalities. Five years later the fires were still burning brightly. And now those flames of love had been brutally snuffed out. Though, she had to admit, now a new fire smouldered within the eyes of Krral . . . a burning desire for revenge.

She sighed deeply. "Krral, sit down. Your pacing makes me nervous. There, that's better. Now, I understand your concern. But being a host for a Questioner is not dangerous and . . ."

Krral leapt up from his chair. "To Brranth piss with danger! I'm not afraid and you damn well know it! I just want to handle this on my own, in my own way. And having some damn alien in my head with me is not my idea of doing things my own way!" He took a deep breath and suddenly his voice became quiet and reasonable. "Look, Urmaal, I know you understand. We'd already discussed this whole thing. It was all set. What happened? Why this sudden change in the arrangements?"

Urmaal gave Krral a considering look. *Now he's trying to act reasonable since all the bluster didn't work. Well,* she admitted, *that's definitely an improvement. How much can I tell him? Enough. Just enough to help him accept and play the role the Service and I need him to play.* She hated doing to Krral what she had to do, but when you were a Third Hundred and a Commissioner, it came with the territory. And then, there were her own personal reasons as well.

She nodded slightly and absently stroked the greying fur on her left arm. That arm still ached when the weather changed. The Medics claimed they had fixed it completely, but it still ached. But then, aches became more common in one's Third Hundred. "All right, Krral, I guess you are due some sort of explanation." Krral sat down again. She planned her approach. *Bluntness. Seem direct, flat, factual. Hit him with facts he doesn't know, can't know. He'll spend so much time thinking about them, he won't notice the gaps until later. And by then he'll be in too deep to pull out.*

She took a deep breath and began. "What neither of us knew at the time of Mraal's death was the fact that she was a host. Mraal was carrying a Questioner when she died."

Krral stared in incomprehension. "She . . . but that's not possible . . . I mean . . ."

Urmaal shrugged. "It was news to me, too. When the Ministry asked for someone for a couple of months of detached service, I gave them Mraal because she wasn't busy and because you were off dealing with that mess on Ranth-urrl-Nimar and she was bored without you around. Her mission should have been cleared up by the time you got back. No one at the Ministry said anything about hosting or Questioners. But whatever they said or just conveniently forgot to mention, that's what happened."

Krral frowned deeply. "But . . . a Questioner here on Ranthar? We have no need of Questioners. That makes no sense."

"Neither does Mraal's murder, Krral," Urmaal said quietly.

The Ranthrr's jaw dropped and a low growl came from his throat. "Murder? Did you say murder?" His voice was deceptively soft and definitely dangerous. Without having to see, Urmaal knew his claws were out.

She nodded slowly, firmly. "Murder."

"But the report declared accidental death in the line of duty."

Perhaps negligence on the part of some Ranth. It said nothing of murder."

"Nor will it ever. Nor will that word leave this office except in your head. Mraal was murdered, Krral. She was stabbed to death."

"Stabbed to death," Krral said tonelessly. The muscles of his shoulders, chest, and upper arms were knotting with tension as if he were getting ready to spring on prey and slaughter it. "Stabbed to death. What . . . was the weapon?"

"A Skrraath sacrificial dagger. She was stabbed the ritual three times in the three vital centers."

Krral growled a deep curse. "The Old Gods. The Old Way. They were serious."

"Very serious, Krral. The dagger was an original, not a copy. A museum piece. Listed as stolen some years ago."

"This . . . changes things, Urmaal."

"I thought it might. That is why I violated direct orders from the High Minister himself and told you. She was your mate. You have Blood Right in this affair, Krral. But the Ministry is not at all keen on the idea of putting a recent Second Hundred Ranthrr on this case. Especially not one who didn't have the best record for stability and calm during his First Hundred when he was a colonist on Ranth-urrl-Urthar and has not exactly racked up a record for self-control in his first five years in the Service. And double especially not when he might take the ancient idea of Blood Right seriously."

Krral looked sharply at her. "I take it seriously. Very seriously. As you did in your time."

She nodded and smiled slightly. "Yes, I took it very seriously indeed. And as a result I very nearly spent the rest of my Second Hundred on Ranth-urrl-Vynnur. And that was when Numrrul was High Minister."

"Yours was the first case of murder for many hundreds of years, wasn't it, Urmaal? Snurrl was murdered, wasn't he?" Krral's voice was soft, his question tentative, as if he were not too sure how she would react.

So many years now, she thought, her mind drifting back to that past. At least a hundred and twenty. And still I feel the anger rise in my heart. The grey in my fur does not mean the fires have died yet. Though there was blood, there was no true revenge. Some day, some day. It is not yet finished. Like an ancient hunting Ranth, I lie waiting, hidden in deep grass.

She brought her attention back to the present and Krral. "Snurrl was the first case in over five hundred years, to be more precise." She sighed. "Like you, I demanded the right to investigate. And because the situation was so unheard of, there were no real precedents to deny me that right. Plus, the High Minister was not unsympathetic." She smiled grimly. "I fear that after what I did, there are now precedents. And they work against you.

"Look, Krral, there's really no sense in snuffling over this trail again and again. The orders from High Minister Shrryl are very specific. You will *not* be assigned to this investigation *unless* you accept to host the Questioner. The High Minister feels it will provide a 'moderating' influence, as he put it. If you want to play this game, those are the rules you'll have to play by." She sat back in her chair. There, she thought, all the cards are on the table. Or at least all I am allowed or intend to lay out. Just enough to make both Krral and the Ministry think they understand the game they are playing.

Krral was thoughtful. "When will this Questioner arrive?"

"Rruml and Tryaal have been sent to Labryinth to request a new one. They took the body of the first one with them in a stasis tank. I do not think they will have any trouble obtaining the services of a new Questioner." She did some quick mental calculations. "Which will mean that within a week or so the Questioner will be here. It will put its ship into orbit around Ranthar. Then it will transfer down into its host. Which will be you?"

Krral nodded grimly. "Which will be me."

"Peace through transcendence."

"Liberation from the Paradox."

"What news?"

"It is as we expected. Another one comes. And Krral will be the host this time."

"Damn. I'd rather it were not Krral. He creates problems we don't need."

"Yes. But he creates equal problems for the Others. Surely you do not fear him?"

"Fear him? Of course I fear him! Only a fool wouldn't fear a Ranthrr like Krral. Especially when his mate has been killed and he'll undoubtedly be seeking Blood Right. He's strong, swift, and his claws are sharp. But more importantly, he's damned intelligent. I'd much rather they'd put some fat, slow bureaucrat on this investigation. Krral might well find out more than is good for us."

"Then he must not learn that much."

"Huh. Try stopping a sandstorm on Ranth-urrl-Gobnar, but don't get in Krral's way."

There was a pause. "Then what happened to Mraal might happen to Krral."

"Easier said than done. And there's also the issue of the Questioner which must be considered."

"The Questioner presented no problem last time."

"That's foolish. The Questioner presented grave problems last time, if for no other reason than that it's led to the presence of another Questioner. And remember, this one will know what happened to the last, just as Krral will know what happened to his mate. No, things are getting out of hand. I don't like this situation one bit."

The voice had an edge of sharpness to it. "Like it or not, the problem is yours to deal with. Master Grrul says the Left-hand Pathway must be protected. At all costs. That is your sole duty and your sole concern. The mere fact that you know Krral has no bearing. Even if you were littermates, the demands of the Master would be the same and your response would have to be identical. What is that response?"

There was a short pause and then a long sigh. "I will obey." Another pause. "But I'll damn well obey cautiously. This isn't a simple issue. The death of Mraal has complicated matters. What role has Urmaal played in all this?"

"It was she who went to the High Minister and asked to have Krral put on the job. It was also she who suggested a second Questioner and that Krral be named host. She has not forgotten nor forgiven Snurrl's death."

"But she cannot know! The very violence of her Blood Right indicates she didn't guess the truth! To kill those fools outright, without questioning a one of them . . . And besides, the trail is so cold by now that no Ranth could follow it."

"We do not know that for sure. As to what she learned from those she killed, we have only her own testimony, which was terse at best . . . and the silent corpses of her victims. Be that as it may, and we are not at all sure she does not suspect far more than she makes apparent, it was she who specifically arranged this assignment for Krral."

"And she who got Mraal assigned to the first investigation. And suggested the original Call for a Questioner. Hmmmm, hmmmmm. There may be even more here than I thought. Damn! This is becoming as tangled as a Skrith web! It's barely begun and I like it less and less. What of the Others? Are they aware of Krral's assignment?"

"It seems likely they would be. It is hard to keep secrets from the Others. They are invisible still in high places, but they are there in growing numbers."

"Scary thought. How long will the Master hold off acting against them? We should strike before their power becomes too great. If they grow too numerous . . ."

"Their disease is more widespread than any realize. Every day its foul contagion touches new Ranth. More even than the unbelievers, they are the true enemy."

"We must steer Krral to them."

"His path will lead him to the Others without our help."

"Do you suggest that it was they who . . . ?"

"I suggest nothing. Merely that when Krral investigates the death of his mate, his path will lead him to the Others."

"Huh. If it does, his path may be a short one."

"Indeed. Peace through transcendence."

"Liberation from the Paradox."


They met in the dark, invisible to each other. The only things that could have identified them were their voices, and those they did their best to disguise. One spoke hoarsely on purpose, the other shrilly.

"Peace and endless sleep," the hoarse voice intoned.

"Endless sleep without dreams," came the shrill response.

"Krral is their choice."

"This is not good news. It means our influence with Shrryl is weaker than we thought. And what of the rumors we have heard of another Questioner?"

"Worse news yet. The answer is yes. And Krral to be host."

The shrill voice cursed. "Then will the next Solution be postponed? I was to be one of the Chosen to participate. Will I have to put it off yet again? How long must this suffering go on?" There was a pause and a deep sigh. "Ah, ah, well, then, this is all but one more proof that the Righthand Pathway is the true way. Those fools who walk the other path did not spend long enough at the crossroads thinking the matter through. They did not follow their logic unto death."

"Krral is dangerous. We would have been better served if they had chosen another. But we clearly failed with Shrryl and there is no way to sway Urmaal. That bitch is immovable."

"Perhaps," the shrill voice said thoughtfully, "the members of the Faction are right and the Solution should be extended even to those who have not chosen it. Especially to someone like Urmaal who causes us so much trouble."

"If it is not chosen voluntarily, if it is not the path freely walked out of the Paradox, then it is not the Solution and the Paradox is not eluded," replied the hoarse voice firmly. "No one can walk the true path in another's paw prints or with another's will. The Solution must be personal or it is as meaningless as the Paradox. I do not agree with the Faction."

"Nor I, nor I," said the shrill voice hastily. "But there are times when one would like to see . . ."

"Like Mraal?"

"Ah, that was clearly a mistake. But whose?"

"Indeed, whose? With Krral on the job we may discover sooner than we would like. I fear this Krral. I knew him all too well during his First Hundred."

"Perhaps something will have to be done about him."

"Perhaps, but let us hope that the Deluded Ones do it, for I have no desire to come up against Krral again."

"And yet it would be your job, would it not? Ah, well, we can only wait and see how things develop. We will meet again at the appointed time. Until then, peace and endless sleep."

"Liberation from the Paradox."

*For the seeker,*
*a single certainty is sufficient.*
*He only has to deduce*
*all the consequences of it.*
          Albert Camus
          The Myth of Sisyphus

Krral nodded grimly. "Which will be me." He sat back in his chair and frowned. "Have we any clues as to who the murderer or murderers are?"

Urmaal shook her head. "Nothing certain to go on. My first thought was that the assignment the Ministry had placed her and her Questioner on might give us someplace to start." She stopped speaking and sat looking thoughtfully off into the distance.

"And?" Krral prompted impatiently.

"And the Ministry refused to comment. Said it was a High Priority mission which could not be discussed."

Krral growled angrily. "Not even to solve the first murder in over a hundred years?"

She smiled humorlessly. "They simply claim the two were utterly unrelated. To quote High Minister Shrryl, the murder was an 'aberrant phenomenon unrelated in any way to the assignment of Operative Mraal.' He was most adamant."

"Brranth piss," he snarled. "That's obviously the place to start searching. It's one of the few certainties aside from the murder itself we have in this case. Besides, this is clearly Service business involved with enforcing the laws of the Ranth. Our jurisdiction extends not only over the colonial worlds but even to Ranthar itself. We have a clear need to know here."

"I fully agree. But the Ministry does not. And Ministry security takes precedence over our jurisdiction and need to know. So you will have to violate Ministry security and find out on your own, won't you?"

Krral's laugh was short and harsh, almost a growl. "Damn right I will!" He paused, a sudden idea flashing across his mind. "Urmaal, was Snurrl on a mission for the Ministry when he was murdered?"

"Yes," came the terse answer. There was a pause for several moments. Then she continued. "And to answer your next question, they said it was High Priority and wouldn't tell me what it was all about."

"But you found out?"

"I found out." The answer was grim and final. Krral knew he would learn nothing more for the moment.

Krral sat back in his chair, musing. "Hmmmmmm. Hmmmmmm. I wonder . . . Urmaal, have you been hearing the rumors of suicides? Back about a couple of years ago, when I first joined the Service, I remember a flurry of suicides that were reported on the datanets. Then everything quieted down and no more was heard of it. Not even a murmur. Until recently. I've been hearing things in various places. Just soft whispers. Of people dying here on Ranthar. Not those at the end of their Third Hundred only. Younger. Much younger. No Departures held for them, either. They just die and disappear. Literally."

Urmaal nodded slowly. "I, too, have heard these whispers." She frowned. "Though I have no remembrance of anything specific coming over our Service datanet about them. Hmmmmm. Are you suggesting that Mraal may have been investigating those rumors? Hmmmm. Suicide and murder. An interesting pair. And an interesting hunch on your part."

She swiveled her chair so that she faced her datanet terminal. Quickly she touched in Subject: then Suicide: and hit the Send key. She stared fixedly at the screen. Then a few seconds later, she reached out again to the keypad, entered her personal code and impatiently struck the Priority Override button three times in rapid succession.

From where he sat, Krral was unable to see the screen. But he could see Urmaal's reaction to what came up. Her eyes widened slightly, then narrowed in a way everyone on the Service had come to fear. That slight narrowing meant the

Commissioner was angry. Very angry. He sat silently, waiting for her to take the lead.

Urmaal finally spun her seat back to face him directly. He raised one eyebrow to frame the question as subtly as possible. A slight frown appeared between her eyes. "Drivel on the first try. A definition of suicide and an official statement pointing out that it was almost unknown in Ranth society, given our high level of medical technology. I keyed in triple priority to cut that foolishness short." She stopped and looked deeply thoughtful, the frown spreading from between her eyes to her whole forehead. "Access was denied."

"Denied? But you're the Commissioner of the Service! How could they deny you access to material like that?" He paused thoughtfully. "Or better yet, why?"

She shook her head. "That's not the issue, Krral. No, it's too obvious. No subtlety. If someone had really wanted to keep me from accessing that information, it would have been much smarter to lead me in tight circles, to throw endless, niggling barriers in my way, to bore and exhaust me. But to flatly deny access is crude."

He nodded. "I see. Then could it be that someone *wants* you to look for that information and assumes this is the best way to get you to do it? Hmmmmm. That seems an equally obvious and clumsy way of going about things."

She smiled again, her expression cold. "No. I don't think they want me to investigate. I think they want you to. As I said, suicide and murder make an interesting pair. Obviously someone else thinks so, too. Your hunch was a good one."

Krral looked thoughtful. "The Questioner comes in a week. That gives me a week to work on my own." He stood with one fluid movement. "I think I'll make it a busy week. Somehow I don't really believe I'm in much danger this early in the hunt. At least not until the Questioner is here. So, while I still have the luxury of being allowed nonlethal errors, I just might do some foolhardy things and get this investigation rolling."

"Like?" Urmaal asked.

"Like breaking into the Ministry and looking up the files on suicides. And on Mraal's mission." He turned and stalked to the door of her office like an animal already on the hunt. "See you when I have some hard info to report," he threw over his shoulder as he left.

"Good hunting," she called out as the door closed. Then she sat back for a few seconds and looked thoughtfully at the door. It begins, she mused. The spoor is down and the hunter on the trail. And this time, she promised, the right game will be run to earth and its bright blood will flow.

I promise it, Snurrl.

# II.

*The mirror of possibility is no ordinary mirror;*
*it must be used with extreme caution,*
*for, in the highest sense,*
*this mirror does not tell the truth.*
> Soren Kierkegaard
> The Sickness Unto Death

It was amazing how easy it had been to get into the central file room of the Ministry. Krral had had to scale one short wall to an air vent, then crawl through a duct network for perhaps fifteen feet until he came to an access hatch. From there he had lowered himself to the floor and walked the rest of the way.

Even the door to the room had the simplest of combination time locks on it. Less than half an hour had been necessary to break the code and swing back the three-inch-thick door. Accessing the necessary data codes had taken a bit longer, but that had not really presented much more difficulty than any of the other tasks. Krral sighed deeply. It just shows, he thought, how lax we have become on Ranthar. There has been no threat of war since the defeat of the Emperor and crime is almost unknown. Why would those who live in paradise become criminals? Everything that could possibly be desired was provided for free.

Krral sat back and sighed again. The hardcopies of the data he had made (on the Ministry's own machines) were spread out on the floor before him. Yes, Ranthar was a paradise planet. The colony worlds were another matter. Most of them were marginally habitable. Ranth-urrl-Urthar, for example, where Krral had spent his First Hundred as a colonist working on the plantations, was a very dangerous place, filled with virulent poisons, a savage flora and fauna, and a weather pattern that was violent and virtually unpredictable. Colonists who failed to stick close to the settlements, or who didn't exercise extreme caution when they left the safe zones, often died. Someday, when the terraforming and weather control projects had been completed, Ranth-urrl-Urthar would be as paradisiacal as Ranthar. But that day was far off.

Krral stretched and flexed his claws. He looked absently at them. They were carefully trimmed and shaped in a fashion which declared him to be a practitioner of the ancient Ranth martial art known as Dreadclaw. His great grandsire, Krral the First, had been a grandmaster of Dreadclaw, and the most esoteric aspects of the art had long been passed down within the bloodline. When Krral had left the pride nursery as a decade cub, he had been taken in by an uncle and drilled endlessly in the art. Being raised by an uncle wasn't the same as having a real mother and father, but old Grrml had been a fine Ranthrr. It had been kind of him to take Krral in after the death of his parents. And to treat his brother's child as if it had been his own.

Krral sat forward and stirred the hardcopies with his foot. It was all there and it didn't make any sense whatsoever. The story went back much further than Krral had suspected. Back at least eighty years. That was when the first suicides had been recorded, though it seemed likely some had taken place well before that. Most Ranth abhorred the idea of suicide and would doubtless have lied about the cause of death of a close relative to avoid the stigma of such a senseless act.

Why commit suicide? Death was long in coming to the Ranth. The average life span, not counting those who died young on the colony worlds during their First Hundred, was about three hundred and twenty-two years. During the first two Hundreds, Ranth were uniformly healthy, thanks to their advanced medical sciences. In the Third Hundred, minor aches and pains began to emerge, but even then, there were medicines and things to alleviate any real discomfort.

Even at the very end of one's Third Hundred, there was no reason to commit suicide. First of all, when a Ranth reached the point of dying, the doctors simply gave him or her an injection and he or she passed away in peace and serenity.

Second, and even more important, Ranth medical research was at the very verge of discovering the secrets of immortality. It could happen at any time, even during one's Third Hundred. Even during one's last decade. Why commit suicide when immortality was just around the corner? Better to hold out to the last minute just in case the breakthrough came.

So suicide made no sense. Yet there it was. Suicide. Or rather, suicides. Many of them, the number growing every year. Eighty years ago it had been one here, one there, a mere scattering, random, infrequent, nothing to deserve any real notice or raise any real concern. But then just five years ago there had been a sudden, dramatic rise in the number and frequency of deaths. That must have been the report he remembered.

He picked up one of the hardcopies and stared at it. And then there was this. Not just an increase in suicides, but a shocking change in their character. Rather than scattered deaths, here, there, everywhere, a new pattern had emerged about a year ago. Mass suicides. Groups of ten to fifteen, all dying together at the same time and in the same place. Even more frightening was the ritual nature of all the deaths. Each of the dead had died as the result of a stab wound, received in the left side next to the heart. Whatever weapon had delivered the wound, it had sliced inward and directly ruptured the heart. Death had been almost instantaneous.

He shook his head. Stupid. Crazy. Senseless. The suicides appeared mainly to be older Ranth near the end of their Third Hundred. But the most recent data showed a few who were only in their Second Hundred. Perhaps on a colony world, where life was often brutal and harsh and dangerous, Krral could understand someone becoming so desperate that they might contemplate suicide. He'd had some pretty tough moments when his first mate, Smaal, had been killed by a Brranth, literally ripped to pieces before he could even come to her aid. He'd killed the Brranth with his bare hands, something no one had ever done before. Afterward, in the medical center on Ranth-urrl-Urthar, where he was recovering from the gaping wounds the Brranth had torn in his flesh, he'd been pretty low. But he'd never seriously considered suicide. How then could you explain Ranth here on Ranthar, where everything they could want was supplied for free, killing themselves?

Apparently no one at the Ministry could explain it either. And that had worried them. So they had gotten an operative from the Service to investigate the problem and see what could be found out. Mraal had been that operative. And what Mraal had found was her own death. Stabbed with a sacrificial dagger.

And Mraal had been host to a Questioner. It was all there. High Minister Shrryl himself had made the decision to send out the Call for the Questioner. It had arrived and joined Mraal in the investigation. Although he could find no indication that Mraal had ever filed a report (which seemed strange, given Service procedures), he could guess the rest. Except the who and the why. Which was all that really mattered.

Krral closed his eyes and slumped back. It made no sense. There didn't seem to be any pattern. Or if there was one, a large chunk of it was simply missing, which made it impossible to discern the rest. But what was missing, if anything? If he could just find the empty space, just understand what was lacking, it would give him a good sense of what the rest of the pattern had to look like. He groaned and leaned forward again to stare at the hardcopies. I'll go through everything one more time, read every word, explore every crossreference. Then I'll put it all away and think about it, let it all percolate down through my mind. Maybe something will happen on the subconscious level, some connection connect, some pattern emerge.

He looked over at the calendar that hung on the wall. Damn! In two more days that stupid Questioner will be here, he thought. Rruml and Tryaal had reported it was on the way. Two more days until I have to share my mind with some alien creature. Two more days to do this thing my own way.

With a low growl, he began reading.

Urmaal frowned down at the report. She raised her eyes briefly to meet Krral's, then returned to the reading. When she had finished her third time through, she slammed the single sheet of paper onto her desk top. "That's it?"

Krral nodded. "That's it. Or at least, that's all I was able to access. There may be more data carefully hidden under exotic passwords, but there's no way to access that in any case."

"It doesn't make any damn sense," Urmaal complained, picking up the sheet again and glaring at it. Krral noted that her canine teeth showed slightly when she glared, giving her a very ferocious appearance. He briefly wondered what she had been like during her First Hundred. The legends of her Blood Right after Snurrl's death were still murmured throughout the Service. He'd even seen some faded pictures someone claimed were photocopies of the originals showing the bodies of the ones she'd revenged herself on. The fur on the back of Krral's neck rose slightly at the memory.

Urmaal put the paper back on the desk top again. Her expression had changed from ferocity to thoughtfulness. "Suicide. On a planet where the possibilities of eternal life are just around the corner at every moment. With that kind of possibility hanging over one's head, why would one kill oneself? If any of them had caught Thrrnn Fever, I could understand it. Although there hasn't been a case of that anywhere on any of the Ranth worlds since early in my First Hundred. But just to kill . . ." Her words trailed off into silent musing.

Finally she brought her mind back to the present and to the Ranthrr who sat across from her. His report, although scanty, had been thorough given the data he had been able to access. He could be fed more with time, but for the moment what he knew was sufficient. She folded her hands on the desk in front of her. "What do you make of the ritual aspect?"

Krral shrugged. "Suggests an organization of some sort. If it was only one isolated group, I'd call it a fluke. But there are five incidents reported. Two from the northern landmass, two from the southern landmass, and one from the archipelago. Techniques were identical. Same wound made by a weapon thrust into the heart from the left side, same position of the bodies. If I didn't know such things had died out millennia ago, I'd almost say it was some kind of cult."

She nodded slowly. Good. He was making good headway. "We should check out the wounds. See if they match the ones on Mraal. By the way, in case you're interested, I checked out that dagger Mraal was murdered with. It was an authentic Ranth Treasure, stolen from a private collector up north about ten years ago." She thought for a moment. "Do you know the last time when daggers like that were used?"

"Yeh. I looked it up in my datanet. It was by this weird cult that flourished during the Expansion, before the First Imperial Wars. The Old Gods were involved. The whole thing seems like a far-fetched charade, except that hundreds of Ranth died.''

"Tell me."

He shrugged. "Not much to tell. Some morons decided that all the problems the Ranth were having then was because the Old Gods were wearing out and needed a transfusion of energy. Seems they'd been ignored for a long time, ever since the Breakup, no sacrifices and that sort of thing. If something wasn't done soon, according to the nuts, the whole universe, starting with Ranthar, was simply going to run down in entropy-death. The only energy suitable for the Old Gods was, of course, Ranth blood. Those fools must have been reading really ancient history from back in the Classical era on Ranthar. They met in groups of twelve, one for each member of the Old Gods' pride, chanted prayers, stabbed themselves in the hearts and bled to death." He growled with disgust. "Almost makes you wonder if we're as sapient as we claim. But then, it was a long time ago."

Urmaal smiled slightly. "Not all that long ago in terms of the race's whole history. We've been around now for a good four million years. Civilized for an easy million. A couple of thousand years is nothing, Krral. The savage hunting Ranth is still closer to the surface than most would like to admit." She flexed her hands, unsheathing her claws and looking moodily at them. "As I well know," she murmured softly.

"Huh," Krral grunted. "I'd admit to hunting Ranth blood any day. But to kinship with fools who stab themselves in the heart so they can revivify the Old Gods . . . well, I'd rather come from a different pride."

She nodded. "I agree. But they saw a possibility for doing something they were convinced needed doing. And possibilities are always enticing. I can almost understand them. But I cannot understand this new bunch. Why are they committing suicide? Have they discovered some new possibility?"

Krral gave her a quizzical look. "New possibility? Are you suggesting they're making some kind of sacrifice to the Old Gods or something like that?"

"I don't know what I'm suggesting. Just that there must be a reason for these suicides. They clearly aren't random. Which is what must have been worrying the High Ministry."

"No, I don't think they're random either," Krral said slowly.

"But so far the only pattern seems to be an internal one. I mean, they all follow the same pattern as far as the act of suicide itself is concerned. But any kind of an external linkage connecting them to a bigger pattern that might show some sense of purpose is still missing. And that's what's bothering me. It's got to exist."

"Hmmmmm. Be more specific. What do you mean?"

"Well, look. A suicide here, a suicide there, even a lot of them, can just be random events. There doesn't need to be any connection between those committing suicide. But this is vastly different. These Ranth did it together like pride members. They must have known each other in some fashion. At the very least they knew that they all wanted to commit suicide. How did they know that? How did they get together? I ran a check on a few of them. No pattern of pride relationship. No pattern of any kind. They look about as much like a random sample of Ranth as one could select. But that's got to be wrong."

Urmaal nodded slowly. "Do a check on the data and commnets of some of the deceased. Find out whom they called and talked with in the last few months before their suicides. Run some correlations to see if you can find a pattern. Maybe some of them talked to the same people. Maybe some sort of links will emerge from that."

"It's worth a try. I've already ordered bios on about ten of them. Five in the most recent group from the northern land-mass, three from the southern landmass, and two from the islands. Maybe something will turn up in their backgrounds that will provide a linkage between them."

Urmaal sat back. He's moving right along, she thought with grim pleasure, just as Mraal did, but much quicker. He has more of the old hunting Ranth in him than most. What will happen when he flushes the first game? Will he end like Mraal? Somehow Urmaal didn't think so. "Not to change topics, but tomorrow the Questioner is due to arrive. Are you ready?"

"Brranth piss!" he snarled angrily. "No, I'm not ready! Damnit, Urmaal, I still think I could do this better on my own."

"I don't dispute that, Krral. But High Minister Shrryl does. It's be a host or be off the case." She wondered briefly if the Questioner would hinder or help Krral. Whichever, she knew he would still stick to the trail until the bitter end. The High Minister just didn't understand this particular Ranthrr if he really thought he could pull him off the case. Blood Right was his, and he would claim it from someone at some time, Questioner or no Questioner.

He growled deep in his chest. "I'll be a host. I'll even try to be civil to this alien. But I'm going to run this investigation my way and no damn four-headed spider snake simian alien had better get in my way!"

Urmaal laughed outright. "Ah, the very picture of Ranth cordiality! 'Four-headed spider snake simian alien!' My, I must remember that one! I believe you have reached a new low in interspecies relations, Krral. For everybody's sake, try to forget that you're a Ranthrr whose second mate has been murdered. Approach this investigation like a professional operative of the Service. Your chances of solving it and surviving will improve markedly if you do."

Krral growled a quiet apology. "Sorry. I'm ready, if not particularly willing. What must be must be. Will the transfer take place at the medical center?"

She nodded. "Yes. At two in the afternoon. Doctor Frryml himself will be officiating." She coughed slightly. "Ummmm, it appears he also handled Mraal's transfer. You'll be given a mild sedative to facilitate acceptance." She held up a hand to forestall his complaint. "Krral, don't bother to tell me you don't need it. I'd wager your hostility index is well over two hundred with respect to this host business. Give the poor Questioner a few moments to get settled before you tell it to butt out."

She paused and gave him a long, considering look. "And, for what it's worth, my advice. Give the Questioner a chance to help. I've got a feeling you're going to need all the help you can get before this is over."

❧❧❧

*Madness is rare in individuals—*
*but in groups, parties, nations, and ages*
*it is the rule.*

Friedrich Nietzsche
Beyond Good and Evil

"Will it be easier for him, or harder?"

"Harder. He has a very strong personality. This sort of thing always works best with those somewhat more malleable in nature. Like Mraal."

"How much control will the Questioner have?"

He shrugged. "It will depend. The Questioner will make no attempt to overcome the host. That is not part of their code. You know what they do? They simply jump at random around the known sphere of inhabited Federation space, checking in at a system to listen for a Call. If they hear it, they go into orbit around the planet giving the Call and then transfer down into a host. Using that host's body and sharing its mind, they simply try to find an answer to the problem posed by the planet making the Call. Their solution is simply their own suggestion. It carries no weight beyond its own inherent value. A Questioner has no authority backing it other than moral suasion. As you can undoubtedly imagine, the role is generally more passive than active."

"Then the idea is to work with the host?"

"That is the idea. Assuming, of course, the host wishes to work with the Questioner."

"But why put a Questioner in a host that isn't willing?"

A shrug. "I can think of several reasons. To punish or

impede the host. To punish or impede the Questioner. To foil the plans of whoever has made the Call. Would you like some more?''

"No, thank you. I take it this host is not as cooperative as the last?"

A harsh laugh. "Do cubs pounce on their own tails? This Krral is not cooperative in any sense. Especially since Mraal was his mate."

"So then he was a bad choice."

"Yes and no. He is a very intelligent, powerful Ranthrr. Something of a throwback. Whoever put him on this case knew what they were doing. They wanted a hunting Ranth, one that would stick to the scent no matter how barren the ground became. And who would spring enthusiastically for the kill when the time arrived. At the same time, the condition attached to the assignment by the High Minister, that Krral be host, poses interesting problems for Krral. And for the Questioner. I have never seen any studies on what happens in the case of rejection by the host personality. But I imagine it would be catastrophic for both.''

"There will be a sedative which *you* will administer?"

A pause. "You are suggesting . . . ?"

"Should the sedative prove to be ineffective, or too weak, or whatever, would it not impede the transfer and perhaps enhance the problems of the host adjusting to the Questioner and vice versa?''

A musing silence. "Indeed it might." Another considering pause. "Such a thing is possible, if not ethical."

"Ethical? Such a word has no meaning in the face of the Paradox. Those who wish to become one of the Chosen must strip their minds of such nonsense. It smells of the Deluded Ones.''

Hastily. "Of course, of course. Such a thing can be done." Thoughtful musing. "A lighter than required sedative dosage. Perhaps even add in something to enhance Krral's natural aggressiveness or reinforce his paranoia. Yes, it could be done. And since I would do the autopsy . . . well, it would be virtually undetectable anyway. Simply one of those unpredictable flukes, an unknown allergy, just one of those unexplainable quirks of medicine.''

"Or simply another proof of the Paradox. Yes, Doctor

Frryml, I think you understand perfectly. It would be a tragic bit of bad luck, to be sure. Perhaps even a fatal one for Krral and for the Questioner. But life is that way and the Paradox is unavoidable. None escape. Very well. Peace and endless sleep.''

"Endless sleep without dreams."

"I tell you, he gained access to the data in the central files and is checking the bios of some of the dead ones."

"That will lead him directly to the Others."

"Not necessarily. Some of that last batch had once upon a time been ours. Any search will come to us first. Damn, I told you Krral was bad news!"

"When will the transfer take place?"

"It's taking place in about an hour."

"Then there is nothing to do except to wait and see."

"We can't afford to wait. We have to act. We have to try and stop this Krral and his damn Questioner before they find out too much. I've made arrangements."

"Arrangements? Explain."

"One of the attendants at the medical center is ours. When the transfer takes place, Krral will be under sedation. Afterward, he will be placed in a recovery room for several hours. Apparently the sedative is necessary to assure the success of the transfer. But while he is still under, she will administer another medicine, one much stronger than the sedative. Are you familiar with Krizzul? Ah, no, eh? It is the venom from a serpent on Ranth-urrl-Gobnar. Nasty little thing. The venom acts very swiftly. It simply stops the heart from beating by interfering with the nerve·synapses in the involuntary system. Then the stuff just disintegrates without a trace. Krral will simply never awake from the sedative. And the Questioner will either be clever enough to withdraw or will die as well."

"That seems rather . . . harsh."

"Damnit, you wanted efficiency! Well, you got it. This is no time to flinch. The best time to stop this thing is before it really gets going. Perhaps we can reach Shrryl in some way and convince him to just drop the whole matter."

"I will tell Master Grrul. I am sure he will be satisfied with your . . . efficiency. Peace through transcendence."

"Liberation from the Paradox."

Krral looked around the sterile, light green room. It felt wrong, menacing. Yet it was a standard room in a medical center, a place of curing and health-giving. He looked at Doctor Frryml who was filling a hypodermic gun with a clear fluid.

The doctor smiled at him. "A mild sedative. Used a thousand times a day on Ranthar. You'll just go to sleep and wake up in about two hours feeling very rested and peaceful."

The attendant came to his side. She was a pleasant-looking Ranthaa with a friendly but professional manner. "Just lie back and relax. I swear, the bigger and stronger you Ranthrr, the more fuss you make over nothing! I'll be in the recovery room with you the entire time. Nothing can go wrong." She smiled and showed him lovely teeth.

He didn't like it. Didn't like the feel of it, the scent of tenseness that clung to both the doctor and the attendant. It reminded him of the way it had felt on Ranth-urrl-Urthar, just moments before one of those insanely violent storms had broken out and devastated everything in its path. Only here the tensions were Ranth rather than atmospheric. He silently cursed himself for a fool. You're making too much of this ancient hunting Ranth bit, Krral, he reprimanded himself. Thinking you can scent the emotions of others. We're past that stage now. We're civilized.

But pheromones are pheromones, a tiny voice declared from the deep past. We cannot control them, even though civilization has taught us how to mask our conscious feelings from view. Whatever your logical mind might tell you, there is danger here. Beware! Beware!

He shot a quick glance over at Urmaal. She seemed calm and collected. Apparently she sensed nothing. But she is old, the little voice harped. Her senses are dulled with age. Trust your own, they are sharp and sure.

Urmaal cleared her throat. "I'm going back to my office, Doctor. Give me a call when he's coming around again. I want to meet this Questioner when it first gets here." She gave Krral a slight salute and left.

Doctor Frryml came to his side with the hypodermic gun. He flashed a jaunty grin at Krral. "Ready?" Krral nodded. No matter his expression, the doctor stunk of fear. Frryml put the gun to his shoulder and pulled the trigger.

Krral blinked twice. His eyes felt very heavy. The attendant loomed over him. "Don't worry," she reassured him with her professional smile. "I'll be there with you the whole time." Her voice seemed to be moving very slowly and coming from an infinite distance. She stunk of deceit as the doctor did of fear. He tried to protest. But before he could even form the words with lips suddenly unresponsive to his demands, he fell into darkness.

# III.

❦

*Beginning to think is beginning to doubt.*
*Society has little to do with such beginnings.*
*The worm lies in each man's heart.*
                    Albert Camus
                    The Myth of Sisyphus

It was like opening a door and unexpectedly stepping into the center of a hurricane–tornado–flash-flood–earthquake–volcanic eruption. Seeker was slammed back and forth, twisted, thrown, battered. The Questioner grabbed the nearest solid thing it could find and hung on for dear life.

*In the name of Labyrinth*, Seeker shouted, *calm down! It's me, the Questioner! You're the host! Try to calm down or you'll destroy both of us!* Fear, rage, worry, fury boiled up and erupted all around Seeker's mind, flinging it about like a tiny craft on a storm-ripped sea. There were cliffs just ahead, cliffs Seeker somehow had to get through or be dashed to pieces at their base. How? How? I've got to reach this host, the ursoid realized, got to get through to its mind. For some reason it's fighting the transfer, trying to keep me out. I've got to make myself heard above this uproar and chaos.

Seeker gathered all its strength, focused its thoughts and blasted straight at the cliffs. DAMNIT! IT'S THE QUESTIONER! LET ME IN OR WE'RE BOTH DOOMED!

The response was hesitant, confused, barely discernible above the howl of the storm. *Questioner? Yes. Mraal dead. Yes. Smell of danger. Questioner. Yes.*

Suddenly the world gave a heave of effort and the resistance was gone. Seeker found itself swept toward the cliffs by a great current. In front of it, a huge portion of the cliff simply split open. With a great whoosh, the Questioner was sucked through the opening and inside.

Something was very wrong. The dreams. The horror. Brranth attacking. Fangs and claws rendinging. NO! The blood. Must fight. Kill! Kill! No. A voice. Let me in! Mraal? No. Dead. Stabbed to death. Daggers slashing down at me. Strike back. Kill the Brranth. Struggle. No. A voice. Damnit! It's the Questioner! Let me in or we're both doomed! Questioner? Yes. Mraal dead. Yes. Smell of danger. Questioner. Yes.

Krral opened his eyes slightly. He felt dizzy and dazed. The attendant was bending over him, a hypodermic gun in her hand. She reeked of death. Without even thinking, he struck out and slapped the gun from her hands. With a small squeal of pain, she leapt back against the wall, her hands covering her face in fear.

Krral struggled to a sitting position. "What were you doing?" he asked, his voice thick and groggy. He unsheathed his claws and waved them menacingly at her. Act tough and dangerous, he told himself. Act like you're about to spring across the room and rip out her throat, even though in truth you probably can't even stand yet. "Damnit! Answer me," he slurred.

"Nothing," she whimpered. "You were so restless. Just a little shot to calm you down. Nothing really. Just standard procedure. Really."

He frowned at her and carefully put his weight on his feet to see if he could stand. He could. Slowly, watching his balance, he bent down and picked up the hypodermic gun. He looked it over. Normal model. Filled with a light green liquid. Could be anything for all he knew. Krral turned his attention to the attendant, who was still cowering against the wall, her eyes very big and frightened. "Normal, huh?" he growled, waving the gun at her and showing his fangs. "Then I suppose you won't mind if I give it to you, huh?"

The wave of fear that came from her was palpable. One didn't need any hunting Ranth senses to know what her pheromones were signaling. "N . . . no . . . please . . ."

He growled deep in his chest and took a slight step toward her. It was almost more than he could manage and he knew it was sheer bluff. But it was enough. The attendant gave a muffled shriek and fainted dead away.

Krral stepped back and sagged against the table he'd been lying on. He was sweating with his efforts and his knees were feeling very rubbery. Got to get my breath, he commanded himself. Now that she's out of the way for a while, I need to take a rest and get my energy back. He looked at the gun in his hand. Whatever it is it must be damned potent stuff, he judged. Might be a good idea to take it with me and find out what it is.

He rested for five minutes. Can't afford any more time, he told himself. No knowing when she'll regain consciousness. Or worse yet, there was no way to tell when that damn Doctor Frryml will come poking around to see how I'm doing. Yeh, doing. That bastard was probably in on the whole thing. He'd been the one to take care of Mraal, too. I'll pay the good doctor a little visit once I've got my strength back, he promised himself. Then, feeling he had recovered enough energy to get out of the medical center under his own power, he went to the door of the recovery room and opened it slightly. He peered through the crack. The corridor outside was empty in both directions. He slipped out.

Urmaal looked up in surprise. "What in pride's sake are you doing here? Doctor Frryml didn't call to tell me you were out from under the sedation yet. What's going on?"

Krral growled deep in his chest as he sat down wearily in the chair in front of Urmaal's desk. He threw the hypodermic gun on her desk. "Got a link to the lab analyzer? Test the Brranth piss in this thing."

Giving him a quizzical glance, she picked up the gun and went over to a small ovenlike machine that was in one corner of her office. She opened a door and took out a sample dish. Then she discharged part of the gun's load into the dish, stuck it back inside the machine, closed the door, and touched several commands into a keypad beside it. She returned to her desk and sat down, fixing Krral with an appraising look. "So tell me."

He shook his head. "Let me get my breath. And wait for the analysis. It will make the telling easier."

A buzzer hummed and Urmaal leaned forward to touch the

keypad on her desk console. For several moments she stared at the screen. Then she gave a low growl. "Brranth piss is right. That gun was filled with pure, undiluted Krizzul! There was enough of a dose to stop the hearts of half the Service! Where in pride's name did you get that damn thing?"

"The attendant had it. She was about to pump it into me when I came to."

Urmaal gawked. "The attendant?" She spun back to her console and punched in some data requests. "I'll run a quick check on her. See if she's . . ." She stopped and cursed.

"Access denied," Krral said bluntly. "Am I right?" She nodded. "Try the good Doctor Frryml."

She did as he requested. The whole screen filled with data. She scanned it quickly. "Nothing unusual. Good, clean record."

Krral scowled. "Hmmmm. I figured he'd be access denied, too. Strange. Why allow access to the file of someone as important as Doctor Frryml and yet deny it to a mere attendant? Urmaal, this thing is getting very bizarre. Someone just tried to murder me."

"Are you sure she knew what she was doing?"

He nodded grimly, remembering the wave of terror that had burst from the attendant when he'd moved toward her with the gun. "She damn well knew what she was doing."

Urmaal grimaced, then turned to her commnet. "Commissioner Urmaal, voiceprint ident. Service priority. Get me the medical center. I want to speak directly with Attendant Fmaal." There was a pause of several moments, then a flat mechanical voice replied. "Attendant Fmaal has checked out for the day. Official status, minor illness. Shall we attempt to reach her residence?"

"Minor illness, my tail stub," Krral snarled. "She's run for cover. There's no sense in trying her den. The bitch is in the brush and leaving few tracks. Damn! I should have gotten to her when I had the chance. But I was just too weak and confused because of the transfer. I . . ." He stopped and stared at Urmaal. "Great Gods of Old! I totally forgot about the Questioner! There was this problem. I don't even know if . . ."

*I'm here, Krral,* said a quiet voice in his head. *Things seemed a bit hot back there so I thought I'd just get out of your way for a while and wait for a more opportune moment to introduce myself. This seems to be appropriate. I am Seeker.*

From Urmaal's reaction, Krral realized the expression on his face must be something to see. "What is it?" she demanded. "Is everything all right?"

"Yeh," he muttered, "yeh, the Questioner is here. The transfer was a success and I'm a damn host. What do I do now?"

Seeker assumed the question was directed to it, so it answered, with a dry chuckle, *First, you relax a little. I had a hard enough time getting here. And you aren't exactly making things any easier now that I'm in place.*

"Relax? Be a bit more specific. Relax what?"

*Well for starters, it would be much easier for both you and Urmaal if you would give me access to the portions of your brain that would allow me to speak through your mouth. I won't interrupt you or hog the show, but talking in your mind only is tiring for both of us and leaves Urmaal utterly in the dark as to what we are discussing.*

"O.K. But I don't claim I know what I'm doing. Is this right?" he asked.

"Perfect," Seeker said. "Thank you. That's much better."

Urmaal gave a start. She stared at Krral with surprise. "Krral, that's your voice, but it isn't your way of speaking at all. The . . . phrasings and intonations are . . . different."

"Indeed," Seeker said. "Allow me to introduce myself, Urmaal. I am the Questioner sharing Kraal's mind. My name, if you wish it, is Seeker."

"What kind of alien are you, Seeker?" Krral growled. "A spider, an ape, a snake?"

Seeker laughed. "Sorry to disappoint you. I'm nothing so exotic. My natural form is not all that dissimilar from your own. I'm an ursoid."

The news mollified Krral. "A bear, huh? Not so bad. At least you're a hunter and a carnivore instead of some tree-swinging omnivore that eats everything from grubs to leaves. What are you, male or female?"

The Questioner paused. "Hmmmmm. Yes, I remember now. You are a bisexual species. Sperm and ovum system of reproduction. Well, I fear I am neither male nor female. I am a Nurturer."

Urmaal looked interested. "Neither male nor female? How

is that possible? The word Nurturer means nothing to us that would resemble a sex.''

Seeker sighed. ''Well, I guess you could call my race tri-sexual. We go through three life phases. The first is Chaser. In that phase we are light and swift, almost able to fly across the Plain in pursuit of game. It is a wonderful time of life. I was called Swift then.'' The ursoid fell silent for a moment in happy reverie.

''The second stage is Catcher. Catchers are far more massive, muscular, heavily clawed, very dangerous and deadly. In that stage we catch the game chased to us by the Chasers and kill it. We are slower then, but vastly more powerful. My Catcher name was Strong.

''Our final stage is that of Nurturer. It is the Nurturers who give birth to the cubs and raise them, telling them the Tales and making them fit to serve the pack. Nurturers are slow and ponderous and are the lifeblood of the pack.''

''Fascinating,'' Urmaal commented, ''but I still don't see how that makes you trisexual.''

''Well, when you have two sexes, each sex provides one half of the genetic background of a new member of the species. It's similar in our case. You see, every Chaser carries six protoeggs. They are in little pouches on the upper back. Each egg carries the genetic heritage of the Chaser and that makes up one third of its total. When the egg ripens, a Catcher takes it from the Chaser and places the fertile egg in its own pouch. Then it adds its genetic third and the egg continues to ripen. When it's ready, a Nurturer comes along and harvests it, placing the egg in its own pouch, adding the final third of the genetic material. Each life stage makes its own contribution. Three life stages, three sexes.''

''Well, you sound more female than male to me,'' Krral grumbled. ''No offense.''

''I'm not offended,'' Seeker chuckled. ''It's really quite meaningless to me. Unless it interferes with the mission.''

Urmaal nodded. ''Perhaps it's time to give the Questioner a briefing. Are you ready, Krral?''

''That really won't be necessary. All Krral has to do is give me access to the relevant memories and I'll know what he knows. That will take a lot less time.''

Krral started slightly, then squirmed uncomfortably in his

chair. "Access to my memories? To all of them? Don't hosts have any privacy?"

"Not all your memories, Krral," Seeker reassured its host. "You Ranth live a long time. I probably couldn't even handle all of your memories without suffering some kind of mental overload. Just the relevant ones. If you simply open up and think about the case, it will all pop up."

Krral nodded reluctantly. "O.K." He leaned back in the chair and closed his eyes. "Here it comes. I'm going to remember all I can from the first moment I heard about this damn case until now. Ready?"

In a few moments Seeker said, "Fine. That's what I need for the moment. Who is this High Minister Shrryl? He seems to be intimately connected with what has happened. Has anyone talked with him?"

Urmaal snorted. "Not likely. Both Krral and I work for Shrryl. We aren't about to question him."

"But *I* don't work for him," Seeker reminded her softly. "I assume it was he who had to authorize the Call for both the first Questioner and the direct request made by Rruml and Tryaal for my own presence on Ranthar. And it was also he who demanded that Krral be the host. I believe Krral and I should interview him as soon as possible."

Urmaal and Krral exchanged veiled glances, their expressions carefully controlled. Then Krral broke out in a huge grin. "You know," he almost purred, "this host business might be kind of interesting after all!"

The High Minister's office was at the very heart of the vast Ministry Building. It was plushly furnished with thick carpets in forest green and the walls were hung with jungle pictures by some of the greatest Ranth Old Masters. Shrryl himself was clearly not at all pleased with the idea of this interview. He glared at Krral and huffily shuffled papers on his desk. "This will have to be brief and to the point, Operative Krral. It is most unusual. I am not used to being questioned by a mere operative of the Service and I've a great deal to do."

"Krral is here only because I am here," Seeker said. "And although it may be unusual for someone to question the High Commissioner, the circumstances seem to warrant it. And, after all, that is my job."

"Humph. I don't agree at all. What circumstances? Be more specific. I haven't got all day."

"High Minister Shrryl," Seeker sighed with mild exasperation, "I have come here all the way from Labyrinth specifically at your request. Is that not true?" Before Shrryl could protest, the Questioner continued. "The first Questioner which was called at your specific request was nearly killed, and the host it was in died. Stabbed to death under very strange circumstances. This host was an operative of the Service investigating a series of very bizarre suicides, again at your specific request. Am I correct so far?"

Shrryl was sitting very quietly now, staring coldly at Krral. "I don't know where you got all this information, but go on. Continue."

"Now there has been a murder attempt on the host of the second Questioner. This host was picked at your specific request." Seeker ceased speaking and stared at Shrryl.

The High Minister shifted uncomfortably in his seat. "What is this? Do you mean someone tried to kill Krral? How? When?"

"At the medical center," Krral rumbled. "Doctor Frryml and an attendant named Fmaal were involved."

Shrryl cursed and spun to his commnet console. "High Minister Shrryl, voiceprint ident, highest priority. Connect me with Doctor Frryml at the medical center. And after him, with . . ." He turned to Krral for the name.

"Don't bother with the attendant," Krral glowered. "She's gone to ground already. She isn't there. Pride knows where she's hiding now."

The High Minister nodded and turned back to the commnet. In a second, the mechanical voice came on. "Sorry, sir, the doctor has left the hospital for the day to go home. He was not feeling well and . . ."

"His home, then. Highest priority!"

Another pause. "Sorry, sir, the doctor does not answer his residence commnet. A check of his door comm indicates he has not come in yet."

"How long ago did he leave the hospital?"

"Three hours, twelve minutes, forty-three seconds."

"Travel time to residence?"

"Average twenty-three minutes."

Shrryl spun back to face Krral. "By all the snows of Vynnur, where the hell is he?"

Krral blinked slowly, looking very grim. "The Questioner and I both think you should try the morgue."

The High Minister's jaw dropped. "The . . ." He spun back to the commnet. "Give me the morgue. Highest high."

A voice came on. "Morgue."

"Shrryl here. Doing a routine check on a Doctor Frryml. Works over at the medical center."

"Not any more. He just came in on a slab."

"Dead?"

"They don't come in here any other way, High Minister. This one is very dead."

"How?" Krral blurted out.

"Damnedest thing. It looks like he was fooling around with this huge dagger. Oddest accident I've seen in a long time. And I see 'em all. He must have tripped and fallen on it. Still in him when they found him. Right in his heart."

# IV.

❧❧❧

"I can't believe Doctor Frryml was involved in anything sinister," High Minister Shrryl declared flatly. He gestured toward the file which filled his datanet's screen. "The doctor's record is impeccable. Not a thing out of place. It'll be a hot day in Vynnur before I begin to doubt a Ranthrr like that."

Seeker was thoughtful. "Frryml was in charge of the transfer of Bilrog to Mraal, too. Isn't it a bit strange he would deal with both?"

Shrryl shrugged. "Not really. He's one of five doctors at the center, so on a purely random basis he had one chance in five in both cases. But more than that, he specializes in psycho-physiological medicine, which increases the odds considerably."

"Could any of the other doctors have handled it?"

"Certainly. They were all competent to handle the task. Frryml was just a little more competent, that's all."

"And yet," Seeker said musingly, "Krral's mind was a maelstrom of fear and panic and hostility. If the doctor was so competent and so versed in things psychological, how could that have been? I wonder if Mraal's transfer was equally as difficult."

"Perhaps transfer to any Ranth mind would be similar, Questioner," Shrryl drily suggested. "We Ranth are a powerful race and once were ferocious hunters. Though we are now quite civilized, the hunter lurks within us." He gave Krral an appraising glance. "In some it lies much closer to the surface than in others."

Krral growled slightly. "I was caught in nightmares. Things chasing me. I had to fight back."

"Is that normal for you, Krral?" Seeker asked.

"Normal? Never happened before that I know of. Except right after that Brranth slaughtered Smaal. Yeh. I had some pretty bad dreams then."

"Well, from my point of view, which is from within your head," Seeker said slowly, "you don't seem particularly unstable or hostile. Indeed, the Krral I'm coming to know and the creature who was battling against me when I tried to transfer seem utterly unlike. How can that be?"

Krral looked pensive. "The High Minister said Frryml was a psycho-physiologist. I don't know much about it, but could there be any drugs which might cause such a mental state? I mean, he had a perfect opportunity to administer something like that in the same shot as the sedative and . . ."

Shrryl abruptly held out his hand. "Come over here." Surprised, Krral rose and came around the High Minister's desk. "Hold out your arm." The High Minister held a tube in his hand. He placed it against Krral's arm and touched a small button on its side. Then he took the tube and placed it in a slot on a small console next to his datanet. "Tied to the analyzer at the medical center. If Doctor Frryml put anything in with the sedative it could still be in your system. I doubt it highly, but it is worth checking if for no other reason than to clear the doctor's good name."

Krral returned to his chair and sat silently watching the High Minister drum his fingers on his desk top. The console buzzed slightly and Shrryl touched the keypad on his datanet console. Data appeared on the screen and he studied it.

When he finally turned to face Krral, his expression was grim and he looked much older than his two hundred and eighty-three years. "Traces of Columar B Prototype."

Krral gave the High Minister a quizzical look. "I'm not a doctor. What's that?"

"A paranoia enhancer."

"I still don't understand."

Shrryl sighed and sat back. "It means that the doctor gave you something that would make you slightly crazy, very hostile, even dangerous. It means the doctor tried to mess up the transfer. And it means this whole thing is out of hand."

"Ah," Seeker said, "and just what is this 'whole thing'? Don't you think it's about time we knew, High Minister Shrryl?"

Shrryl stared at Krral with a stony impassivity. Then he sighed and his expression turned to one of worry. "It's hard to get used to talking to two people in the same body. It's really quite odd the way Krral changes when you're speaking, Questioner. Changes and yet is the same.

"Well, well, yes. This whole thing. I fear I really shouldn't have used that phrase. Not a fortuitous phrase at all. At least not at this early juncture. But once the game has been pulled down it must be eaten. So."

He paused as if gathering his thoughts. "This whole thing is as Krral has already guessed. Suicide. Not just one or two, but hundreds. And the number is growing by the month. We haven't a clue as to what is going on, but whatever it is, it is rapidly reaching almost epidemic proportions. Quite simply, we are worried. Quite worried. It makes no sense whatsoever."

"And why not?" Seeker asked. "I know Krral has already told me what he thinks, but what about you, High Minister? Why is suicide so unthinkable?"

Shrryl was obviously embarrassed and flustered by the question. "Well . . . but, I mean, to kill oneself . . . it just isn't the sane thing to do."

Seeker shrugged. "Sane thing to do? Perhaps not. But it seems a lot of Ranth might deny that. Unless you are suggesting that the suicide epidemic is really just the outward manifestation of a real epidemic of insanity."

"Certainly not! I mean, it's crazy to commit suicide, but that doesn't mean . . ." He stopped abruptly, realizing he was caught in a contradiction.

The Questioner smiled slightly. "If suicide is insane and there is a sudden rash of suicides, then it follows that there is a sudden rash of insanity. The logic is rather elementary. Unless, of course, one decides that suicide may not be insane after all."

"But it is!" Shrryl blustered suddenly. "It . . . must be! This is Ranthar! Who could possibly want to commit suicide when they live in a paradise?''

"I don't know," Seeker replied softly. "And that's really what you want us to find out, isn't it?''

The High Minister nodded slowly. "Yes. We must get to the root of this as soon as possible. It must be stopped.''

"Those are two different goals. I take it the first is our concern and the second will be yours.''

Krral broke in. "The High Minister is right. Suicide is crazy. All Ranth know that. And yet there's a rash of it, so there must be a rash of craziness as well, as the Questioner suggests. Maybe we should check the datanet and see if there is any report of an upswing in mental instability here on Ranthar.''

"Good idea," Shrryl said as he swung back to his console and touched commands into the keypad. He turned the screen so that Krral and Seeker could see the information as it glowed to life. They went through the file fairly rapidly because it was short and sparse. "Damn," Shrryl grunted in annoyance. "No increase in psychological problems at all. In fact, it looks like a decrease if anything.''

Krral nodded agreement. "A definite decrease just within the last few years. That's the same period when the suicides were increasing. Odd.''

"Indeed," Seeker commented. "It also cripples the theory that suicide and insanity are related. Or at least that a Ranth would have to be crazy to kill him or herself.''

"But, damnit, it is! It's so crazy we Ranth even have trouble talking about it. If you check the death reports of most of those we know committed suicide, you'll almost universally find the cause of death listed as accidental. Suicide just doesn't take place on Ranthar," Shrryl protested vehemently.

"Didn't," Seeker corrected. "Things have changed.''

Frowning deeply, Shrryl opened his mouth to reply. Krral held up a hand to forestall the High Minister. "May I use your datanet? I've got an idea. I was running a check on those who had died most recently. Provided all the information isn't 'access denied,' it should be ready now.''

"Just a minute," Shrryl said. He touched in some commands. "There. No more access denied. I've given you Status Two.''

Krral nodded acknowledgement and keyed in his request.

The data came up on the screen and they watched it as it scrolled by. After staring at eight case studies, the two Ranth sat back quietly and stared at each other, ignoring the data that continued to scroll up the screen. "Not a damn thing," Krral muttered. "Just a few of them taking mild drugs for tension. Could just as easily have been job-related anxiety. Certainly nothing to commit suicide over."

"Which gives us two possibilities," Seeker proposed. "First, that suicide and insanity are not at all related. Or second, that the onset of the insanity, or whatever form of mental aberration we are talking about, is very sudden and the suicide follows quite swiftly, giving little or no time for it to appear on the medical records of the Ranth who kill themselves. Sadly enough, we don't have enough data to decide on either choice. Krral, now that your access is back, what about the attendant, Fmaal? Perhaps there's something in her file that might help you find her. It might be very interesting to talk with her."

Krral growled softly. "I'd love to do more than talk to that particular Ranthaa." He unsheathed his claws, then realized he was in the presence of his superior, the High Minister, and with a mumbled apology, pulled them back again and placed his hands in his lap.

The High Minister called up the data and they all studied it. "Strange," Shrryl finally said. Krral nodded.

"How so?" Seeker asked.

"Well, I would swear there has to be more information on her First Hundred. Look. She served on Ranth-urrl-Gobnar as a medical attendant after studying medicine there. But there is no listing of the center she served at, nor of the names of the doctors who provided her recommendations for return to Ranthar. That's very unusual."

"Could the file have been tampered with?"

Shrryl shrugged. "It's possible, but hardly likely. Access to the codes for file entry or deletion are very limited. We could trace who has her access. Hmmmmmm"—he touched commands into the keypad—"let's see . . . yes, here. A Third Hundred Ranth named Xrrul in Records." He touched the keypad again and pulled up Xrrul's file on the display. "Hmmmmmm. Yes. Served his First Hundred on . . . huh, Ranth-urrl-Gobnar. Second Hundred in the Service, not a very distinguished record. Third Hundred entered into Records and . . ." Shrryl stopped and then cursed. "Damnit!"

Seeker leaned forward. "Yes? What's the matter?"

"He's dead. Died about a year ago. Coronary complications. Very sudden. Another dead end."

"Literally," Seeker commented drily. "But not quite. It seems that some Ranth who deal with this attendant Fmaal meet with unfortunate accidents, like falling on a dagger, or having a sudden fatal sickness. Including, very nearly, my host, Krral.

"Krral, is there any way to see if she might have gone back to Ranth-urrl-Gobnar? Or wouldn't that be a good place to hide?"

Krral growled a sharp laugh. "It would be a wonderful place to hide. Ranth-urrl-Gobnar is a mining planet, mostly desert, sparsely inhabited by some very independent First Hundred Ranth and a handful of Second Hundred Ranth who don't want to come back to Ranthar because they like the freedom of the most primitive colony we have. Terraforming has barely begun there, Questioner. Ranth-urrl-Gobnar is a pretty rough place. Yes, it would be a very good spot to hide, especially if you already had friends there to help you."

Shrryl nodded in agreement. "Let's put her code into the datanet and check it against boarding on the liners going to Gobnar. Hmmmmm. No. Nothing. No sign of her using her code to book passage. She must still be here."

"Could she have used somebody else's?"

The High Minister considered. "Could have. Not really done. No need to. Everyone has free access once they enter their Second Hundred. Code use is for control, not for financial reasons. But she could have, if she wanted to cover her tracks."

Krral snarled. "She wants to cover her tracks, believe me! Is there any way to find out if she used someone else's code?"

Shrryl considered. He brought some data up on the screen. "Only two liners have left in the last twenty-four hours. She would have to have been on the second one, which left four hours ago. So"—he touched the keypad—"let's call up the codes of those on board. Hmmmmm. Yes. She's not there. So. Next, let's put in Top Priority calls to all those listed."

"Top Priority calls? But they're all gone . . ." Krral paused, suddenly understanding: "Ah, except one of them, if the Questioner is right."

The High Minister nodded. "Yes. One of them should be reachable. Hmmmmm. That one is out. And that one. That one. That one. Ah, what's this? Connection. With one Rrull over in Records. Interesting. I've canceled the call, but Rrull is there, even though he's listed as being on his way to Ranth-urrl-Gobnar." He sat back and looked at Krral. "The Questioner was right. She must have used his code."

Krral stood. "High Minister, if I could trouble you? Would you please print out Rrull's file on my machine over at Service HQ? I want to pay him a quick visit before I go to Ranth-urrl-Gobnar to talk to Fmaal."

"No trouble at all. But if you'll wait a few minutes, I'll have it run out for you here."

"No," Krral replied, "I'm on my way to the morgue."

High Minister Shrryl blinked with surprise. "The morgue? Whatever for?"

Krral shrugged. "The Questioner wants to see Frryml's body. A hunch, it says. And I'm beginning to trust my ursoid companion's hunches."

The attendant at the morgue was a little confused. " 'May we see the dagger?' What 'we'? There's only one of you."

Krral smiled slightly. "Just a way of speaking. Typical of operatives in the Service. We generally work in pairs, you see. Sorry. I didn't realize you were such sticklers for grammar here at the morgue. Since most of your customers don't talk at all. So, then, may *I* see the weapon?"

The attendant sniffed. "Certainly. It's over here." She stepped to a filing wall and touched a keypad. A small drawer slid out. Inside was the dagger. She lifted it out and handed it to Krral. "Careful. It's razor sharp."

Krral studied the dagger. It was about fourteen inches long and resembled the letter S. The blade, rather wide in the center but narrowing suddenly at the tip and near the haft, was sharply curved upward. The hilt curved downward. "How was it found in the body? I mean, how was it situated?"

She frowned. "Situated? Well, it was like you're holding it. Curve of the blade up, hilt curve down."

Krral turned the dagger until it was pointed at his own chest. "Careful," the attendant said nervously. "That's the kind of thing the corpse was doing before he tripped."

"Odd," Krral observed. "This is a very awkward way to hold a dagger. You either have to twist your wrist around at a very acute angle or hold it this way in the hand so that the curve of the hilt goes against the shape of the hand."

*Ask to see the corpse,* Seeker suggested, speaking only in Krral's mind.

"Can we . . . I mean, I see the corpse?"

The attendant gave him a suspicious look. "I suppose so," she admitted grudgingly. "Your credentials are all in order. Not much to see. Just a dead Ranthrr with a hole in his chest. But if you want to, come this way."

They walked down a well-lit corridor to a room with forest green walls. The attendant consulted a chart on the wall, then touched some numbers into a keypad on the wall and a small square on the far wall opened. A drawer rolled out. On it was a body.

Krral walked over and looked down. It was Doctor Frryml. He bent closer to look at the wound. It was actually a little below the heart. From the looks of it, the knife had entered at about a forty-five-degree angle upward.

*Krral,* Seeker urged softly, *do you notice anything strange about the wound?*

The Ranth shrugged. He turned to the attendant. "The wound. Anything strange about it?"

She shrugged too. "Strange? No. The dagger pierced the dermal layers at a point about four inches below the heart. Angle of entry was about forty-seven degrees north/south, about ten degrees east/west. The curve of the blade, plus the angle of entry brought the point directly into the left ventricle of the heart from below. A massive trauma resulted with concomitant internal hemorrhaging and resultant death. He died very quickly. His heart literally came apart."

*Krral,* Seeker said, *you've held the dagger. How would you have to hold it and fall on it to receive a wound like that one? Try to imagine it.*

Krral tried. He tried again. Then he attempted to act it out, pretending to hold the dagger in first his right, then his left hand. He twisted himself about, imagined tripping and falling. It didn't work.

*That's right, Krral. The tendency is to put your hands out when you trip and fall forward, not twist them around toward your body. And even if you wanted to commit suicide by falling on the dagger, you still couldn't fall on it that way. There's only one way a wound like that could have been received. Someone swung the dagger up from below and to Frryml's right. The good doctor didn't have an accident, Krral. And he didn't commit suicide, either. He was murdered.*

Krral nodded slowly. It was obvious now that the Questioner had pointed it out. Like Mraal, Frryml had been murdered, stabbed to death with a dagger. The blow had come from below and to the victim's right, delivered by someone who was left-handed. It had probably come suddenly and unexpectedly. Somehow Krral knew that if he checked, the dagger would prove to be a copy of an ancient sacrificial dagger.

He knew something else, too. He was going to have to watch every step he made, keep his eyes open for any movement in the brush, his nose to the wind, his ears fully extended for the sound of a footfall. He wasn't just the hunter any longer. He was also the prey. Because this wasn't just a question of suicides. This was a question of murders. And if he wasn't very cautious, he would end up a victim of one of them!

Urmaal looked up as Krral entered. She shuffled among the papers on her desk, found what she was looking for, and handed a sheaf of papers to him. "Came in while you were gone. File on some Ranthrr named Rrull over in Records. I took the liberty of scanning it. Nothing much of interest."

Krral sat and skimmed the file. "Huh. This is interesting. Served his First Hundred on Ranth-urrl-Gobnar. Strange co-incidence, that," he muttered sarcastically. "I'm beginning to dislike that planet even though I've never been there."

"Hmmmmm. Ranth-urrl-Gobnar. Odd. Isn't that where your ex-mate, Mraal, started out?"

"Pride's honor," Krral cursed softly. "You're right. I'd completely forgotten about that. She was educated there. Extraction technology of some kind. Then she transferred suddenly to Ranth-urrl-Urthar."

"Strange to transfer like that in your First Hundred. Did she ever say why?"

He shrugged. "Never said. Never came up. But it doesn't seem that strange to me. Ranth-urrl-Gobnar is a hellhole compared to Ranth-urrl-Urthar."

Urmaal gave a laugh. "Ha! Urthar is every bit as bad as Gobnar and you know it! Just an issue of whether you prefer your hellhole hot and dry or hot and damp." She paused. "Any connection between this Rrull and Mraal?"

He frowned as he looked at the file. "Dates are about right. But Gobnar's a big place. Odds would be against it. Still . . . there are an awful lot of coincidences that seem to be centering on Ranth-urrl-Gobnar." He dumped the file on Urmaal's desk and stood. "I think maybe I'll pay a visit to Gobnar. Looks like Fmaal may have gone to earth there. And I really want to have a little chat with her. Could you set up passage for me?"

Urmaal turned to her commnet and touched up the liner schedules. "Huh, think I'm your damn secretary? Here. There's a liner leaving tomorrow morning at eight. Shall I book you, sir?" she asked sarcastically.

Krral smiled. "Yeh, sweetie. Private cabin."

"As you would say, Brranth piss! You're a Service operative, mister. And that means you travel steerage! There, you're booked. Your incognito is a mining equipment specialist working for Tech. Name of Qurrl. I'll have a profile sent to your datanet at home. Be sure you study it."

"O.K. Well, I'm off to visit a friend of mine who works in Records. Going to pay good old Rrull a social call and have a friendly, little chat."

Urmaal laughed again. "Don't hurt him too badly. It won't look good on your record."

He was up against the wall and the claws were only inches from his eyes. Krral growled deeply, the rumble coming from low in his chest. "I don't give Brranth piss about your rights, Rrull. You answer my questions or you'll be discussing your damn rights with the attendant at the morgue. And she's a real stickler for grammar, so watch how you say things."

"You can't just . . ."

The growl became a menacing snarl and the claws touched Rrull's eyelids. "Stuff that crap! I can and I am. You're up to your neck in Drrall shit, Rrull. And if you don't start purring real fast, I'm going to shove you under! Now talk!"

Rrull was shaking badly. He swallowed several times in an attempt to wet his mouth and throat. "I . . . yes, all right, I gave her my code to use."

"Why?"

"She said she didn't want anyone at the center to know where she was. Some doctor was hassling her, trying to bed her, and she just wanted to get away for a while, go back home and relax. You know how it is."

"I don't know how it is. That's the dumbest, stupidest story I've ever heard. Why did she come to you?"

"We . . . know each other."

"From Gobnar?"

Rrull looked surprised. "Why . . . yes. We both were there for our First Hundred. We served . . ."

"Know anyone named Mraal?"

"N . . . no."

"So you knew Fmaal from Gobnar. She has this doctor chasing her and wants to go back for a few days and comes to you for your code, right?"

He nodded eagerly. "Yes, yes, that's exactly what happened. I swear on pride's honor." Krral loosened his grip and began to step back, growling slightly. Rrull breathed deeply with evident relief.

Suddenly Krral slammed his closed fist into the side of Rrull's head, knocking the Ranthrr to his knees. Before he had time to protest, Krral hit him again and knocked him flat on the floor. Then he bent down and grabbed him by the front of his harness and dragged him erect once more, slamming him against the wall three times in the process. "You disgusting pile of simian shit!" he snarled. "You lie to me like that again and I'll rip out your throat! Now tell me the truth before I lose my very short temper. The truth!"

Rrull was blubbering with fear. Blood was pouring from his nose. "I'm bleeding!" he wailed. "I need medical help!"

"If you don't start telling me what I want to hear, medical help isn't going to do you any good." Krral hit him again.

Whimpering, Rrull began to talk. "Fmaal was my mate on Gobnar during our First Hundred. When we came back to Ranth, we split up because she was involved with this group. Something called the Lefthand Pathway. I went to one meeting, but they seemed like a bunch of nuts to me. We had a fight over it and she split. I hadn't seen her in a couple of years. She came to me and she was very frightened. Said somebody might want to kill her. I had to help. It was easy; all I had to do was give her my code so she could book passage on the next liner to Gobnar. She promised there was no danger to me. Then she . . . I . . ."

Krral released him with a disgusted snort. Rrull slumped against the wall, weeping softly. "Yeh. I know. Then she dragged you down on the floor for some good sex and you said yes while you were all hot. Know what you are, Rrull? You're a carrion-eating slime. A damn kitten still sucking at its mommy's teat." He exposed his claws again, waving them at Rrull. "Your story is more believable this time. But give it a second to sink into your own mind. Decide if it's truly true. Evaluate it carefully. 'Cause if one word is out of place, if one comma is missing, I'll be back to rearrange your face with some really interesting scars, buddy."

*What do you think, Questioner?* Krral asked silently.

*He seems properly cowed. At least enough so that I suspect as much as he has told us is true. There may well be more he is not telling, however,* came Seeker's thoughtful reply. *By the way, Krral, I fear your methods lack a certain . . . finesse. Was it really necessary to be so rough?*

*Yeh. I've been told that before. My method's rough. But it's fast and effective. Fear seems to be a good way to convince someone you mean business. Especially slime like this slippery little Ranthrr. In any case, it's my way.* His tone was defensive and slightly belligerent. Seeker decided it was wisest not to press the issue.

"It's . . . the truth. I swear. Truth," Rrull blubbered. "I don't know anything else. I'm not lying."

"Sure. I trust you like a littermate." Krral gave him an appraising look. "I'll be back, buddy, once I've had a chance to verify your story. Think about that."

With a last disgusted look at the whimpering Ranthrr slumped against the wall, Krral turned and left.

# PART TWO

❧❦❧

## *The Logic Unto Death*

# I.

❧ ❦ ❧

*Both the rational and the irrational
lead to the same understanding.
Truly, the path travelled matters little;
the will to arrive is enough.*
                        Albert Camus
                        The Myth of Sisyphus

The system which the Ranth inhabited consisted of a tight cluster of four suns which revolved around a common center. The whole system was about four light years across. Three of the suns had planets. The fourth was a white dwarf which apparently had never had any. Between them, the three planetary systems had eight habitable worlds. Two, including Ranthar, were in the home system. The star nearest Ranthar's sun had four, two of which were only marginally habitable. One of these was Ranth-urrl-Gobnar.

Ranth-urrl-Gobnar was a desert planet with no open bodies of water anywhere on its surface. Its atmosphere was thin, with little free oxygen, since most of it was bound up in oxides on or below the surface. It was possible for Ranth to walk the face of the planet, provided they walked slowly and kept activity to a minimum. Strenuous activity or long stays required some form of oxygen supplement, either in the form of a breather pack or oxygenation tablets. Neither was satisfactory for more than a few days at a time.

But even more than the lack of oxygen, the surface of the planet itself kept Ranth presence there to a minimum. Ranth-urrl-Gobnar was a dangerous place. Despite the thinness of the atmosphere, huge sandstorms were a common occurrence. Sometimes they covered whole continents and raged for weeks on end. At such times, the force of the wind-driven sand became so great that even the toughest protective suit was rapidly abraded away. And nothing could keep the fine dust whipped about by the wind from entering everything and making breather packs and machines alike useless. When the storms finally stopped blowing, the landscape was utterly transformed and unrecognizable, entire sand and gravel mountains having disappeared or appeared without apparent order or reason.

Despite the hostility of the environment, there were both plants and animals living on the surface. The plants were small and low growing, sprouting quickly wherever the winds scoured the land down to the underlying bedrock. They grew in cracks and crevices where they could send down deep roots to suck up moisture that hid in secret underground pools. They grew quickly, between the storms, and then sent their seeds scurrying along with the sand once the winds began to blow.

The fauna of Ranth-urrl-Gobnar was limited and primitive. There were several species of insects that fed on the plants, laying their eggs in the seeds so they could move with their food source. Then there were two species of arachnids that fed on the insects. Though less than a fourth of an inch in length, the arachnids emitted a poison when they bit, a bizarre protein, that was inevitably fatal for the Ranth. It coagulated their blood almost instantly. Finally, at the very pinnacle of the food chain, there was a creature rather like a centipede that fed on everything. It was about a foot long, very aggressive, and extremely poisonous. Worse yet, it had the occasional habit of traveling in groups of several dozen for reasons that appeared to have something to do with its breeding habits. More than one Ranth unlucky enough to encounter a pack of these creatures had left its bones to decorate the surface of Ranth-urrl-Gobnar.

Someday the Ranth terraforming project would transform the surface of the planet and make it into a paradise. The oxygen locked beneath the surface was estimated to be sufficient to create an atmosphere almost as rich as that on the home planet, once it was freed. And surprisingly enough, the amount of subsurface water that dripped and bubbled through the vast caverns beneath the dry, windblown surface would be adequate to support a fairly complex ecosystem once it was drawn up. How long would such a task take? A thousand more years at least. But then, for the Ranth, that meant only three more lifetimes until the promise of paradise was fulfilled.

In the meantime, most Ranth life on Gobnar was conducted below the surface, in the caverns where they lived and the mines where they worked. For the planet was as rich in minerals as it was poor in life. Indeed, the prosperity of every Ranth world was heavily dependent on the rich resources dug from one of the most desolate and inhospitable of them all.

Ranth-urrl-Gobnar was a strange mix of life and death.

The Ranthaa who was head of the Service on Gobnar shook her head doubtfully. "The name doesn't mean anything to me. And we don't do any kind of passenger check to see who gets off the liners from Ranth." She chuckled drily. "No one comes here for the fun of it, so there's no reason to keep tabs. Your Fmaal would have arrived about a week ago and could be anywhere on the planet by now."

"Would she need to use her code to travel?" Krral asked, feeling his sense of frustration grow.

"No. There's no control on travel. Again, Ranth don't just wander around Gobnar at random. They're here for a purpose, so there's no real reason to keep tabs on them."

"Fmaal had a purpose, all right," Krral growled. "She wanted to disappear for a while and it looks like she came to the right place to do it."

"If she spent her First Hundred here, she probably knows the place pretty well. It wouldn't be all that difficult to find a hidey-hole and pull it in after her. Ranth here on Gobnar are pretty clannish and very tight-lipped. They generally don't have much to say even to each other. And to strangers, well, if silence were truly golden, this would be the richest planet in the system."

Krral gave a surly growl. "Well, at least I want to take a look at the file for her First Hundred. Maybe it will give me a clue as to where to start looking."

"Coming right up." The Ranthaa turned to her datanet and touched in the request. She waited a moment as several lines appeared on her screen and she read them. "Strange," she finally murmured, "there doesn't seem to be any file. Are you sure of your facts? Fmaal is the name for certain?"

Krral gave a low curse. "Again! My little attendant is a very slippery Ranthaa. Check to see how many Ranthaa left here for Second Hundred duty on Ranth in the category of medical attendant. Make the search for the last twenty years.''

A few minutes later, they had a list of seven names. All but one checked out. That one could not be traced and no record of her First Hundred file could be found. Krral sat back with a satisfied rumble. ''That's our little lady. Real name is Ymaal. Where is this center she served at? 'Terminus'? Strange name.''

''Not when you get there. It's the last stop on the line, the furthest outpost of Ranth settlement on Gobnar. Nothing but a series of connected caverns that actually open out onto the surface. It's in the southern hemisphere, which if anything is even more desolate than it is around here in the north. Mine a lot of lithium and molybdenum. And, yeh, it's also got the biggest find ever of Eyes.''

''Eyes?'' Krral asked, knowing it was expected of him.

''Eyes of Gobnar. Jewels. Very rare and very beautiful. Most of them are traded off-planet to Federation traders who are willing to pay a bundle for them. Lots of strange stories about them and what people will do to get them. My favorite is the one about the Emperor. Seems he had the biggest one ever found set as the center stone of his imperial crown. Damn thing cost two billion imperial credits at that time. Probably worth three times that now. They claim that's what he went back for when they caught him. If he'd left it behind, he'd have got clean away. But there he was, wandering around the palace in a daze, looking for that damn crown, when they caught him.'' She paused. ''Some people even claim they have some sort of mystical powers. I've only seen one of them. You'd swear the damn thing was alive. Almost seemed like a real eye, staring and staring at you. A little unnerving. Very odd and very impressive.''

''Lithium, molybdenum, and jewels with mystical powers. Huh. Strange combination.'' Krral stood. ''Well, if you'll point me to the right tube, I'll be on my way to Terminus.''

She looked down at her desk top for several moments. Finally she raised her eyes to meet his. ''Be careful, Operative. The Ranth out in Terminus are a queer lot. Some say it's because they live so close to the surface. Some claim its the effects of the Eyes of Gobnar. Whatever, they aren't particularly hospitable sorts. Pride's honor, they're downright hostile, even to other Ranth from Gobnar. No telling how they'll act toward an off-worlder. Especially an off-worlder on the trail of one of their own. Hunt lightly, Operative. Hunt lightly and sleep even more lightly. 'Nuff said?''

Krral frowned slightly. "Any Service contact out there? Just in case?''

She shook her head slowly. "Not any more. Haven't filled that post since the last one died.''

"Died?" Krral asked tensely. "How?''

She shrugged. "Story is he got out on the surface by mistake and the centipedes got him. The one before that got bit by a damn spider that snuck down into the caverns. Or so the story goes.''

Krral was silent in thought. Finally he asked, "How long since the post's been empty?''

"About four years. I'm afraid you're on your own, Operative. Very much on your own.''

Of the five Ranth who shared his compartment between Gobnar Center and Leadville, only one was the least bit talkative and coincidentally, that one was also going to Terminus. The Ranthrr from Terminus was a First Hundred miner named Trrulul. He also occasionally went out prospecting for Eyes. He'd found two so far, of middling size. "But someday I'll find a nexus, you wait and see. Then I'll be rich, by my pride's honor!''

Krral was curious. "Rich? Why do you need to be rich? Don't you have everything you need?''

Trrulul gave a harsh laugh. "Everything? Here on Gobnar? On Gobnar, friend, one is lucky to have barely enough.''

"But what would you do with your wealth? Import things to Gobnar, to Terminus, to make your life better? But why? Surely it's not that long until your Second Hundred. Then you'll be back on Ranthar and it will all be unnecessary.''

The miner frowned deeply. "With wealth, I could buy my way back to Ranthar without havin' to wait for my Second Hundred. Don't deny it. It can be done. Turrl did it when he found that nexus. He was gone in a month, they say. Someplace on Ranthar now, basking in the sun, drinking all the water he wants, eating his fill, nice, soft Ranthaa to satisfy his every whim. Ha! I know about these things. We all do.''

Krral shrugged. The Ranthrr was talking nonsense. But he

was big and burly and patently hostile, so there was no sense in disagreeing. Hunt lightly, he reminded himself. *Yes, please,* Seeker added silently. *This chance meeting with someone going to the same place you're going would seem like mere coincidence if it weren't for the things that had already happened. I don't trust this Ranthrr. Hunt lightly indeed!* Krral agreed silently.

The miner fixed him with an inquisitive eye. "So why are you bound for Terminus? Comin' for the luxurious resort accommodations?" He sputtered into deep, raucous laughter. "Ha! Ha! You got to try the mineral baths!" He roared at his own heavy humor.

Krral smiled politely. "Nothing so exciting. Looking up an old friend from academy days. One fine little Ranthaa named Ymaal. Know her?"

Trrulul frowned with concentration. "Ymaal? Hmmmmmm. What'd she do? Not a miner, huh?"

"No. Med."

The miner shrugged. "Oh, med. Well, I'm never sick so I never meet any of them med types. I'll stay away from the meds if they'll stay away from me is what I say! Healthy Ranthrr don't need no meds. Ymaal? Cute, you say, huh? Maybe I'll look her up once you're gone, friend. What'd you say your name was?"

"Qurrl. Work in Tech."

"Qurrl," he rolled the word in his mouth as if savoring it. He nodded. "Good, honest name, that. And Tech is a good, honest place to spend your time. Tell you what, Qurrl, if you've a mind to it, while you're in Terminus, just look me up. We'll go have a bit to drink and I'll introduce you to some of the other miners. A good lot. Mite rough, mind you"—he leered slightly at Krral in challenge—"but a good bunch all the same. Maybe if we take a shine to you, we'll let you come on an Eye hunt with us. That is, if you aren't afraid of goin' out on the surface. Who knows? Beginner's luck might do us all a good turn, huh?" He chuckled deep in his throat.

When they arrived in Terminus, Trrulul pointed Krral in the direction of the closest lodging and went rolling off for a "little drink with the boys."

*It is not so much identical conclusions reached
that prove minds to be akin,
rather it is the contradictions
that they share.*

Albert Camus
The Myth of Sisyphus

"He is the one for certain?"

"No question. I'd stake my next nexus of Eyes on it. He smells of the Service and of Ranthar like a centipede smells of death. Arrogant bastard."

"Hmmmmm. And he knows that Fmaal and Ymaal are one and the same. We must check the records again. Obviously we slipped someplace. All trace must be eliminated."

"Not my job." A pause. "Couldn't tell if he had a Questioner with him or not. That's the part I don't like. Him, huh, he's nothin' but a soft fool from Ranthar. But a Questioner, well, who knows what that means?"

"The Questioner I can't give you any advice on. It's a completely unknown factor. But I can advise you not to underestimate Krral. He is anything but soft. And don't forget it was Urmaal who set him on this trail."

"That bitch again! We should terminate her."

"Nothing so harsh. Master Grrul will not even consider it. Snurrl's death continues to radiate out like ripples from a stone thrown in an underground pool. The death of Urmaal would cause more than just ripples."

A snort. "And how about that last Service operative? The one who 'wandered' out on the surface by mistake? Seems to me this one is likely to make a similar mistake."

"The last one was unfortunate. But he came too close. I suspect he was set on us by Urmaal. She has a trace of the scent, though the shifting of the wind keeps her unsure of the location of her prey. We must be more cautious than ever. I don't like the fact that no new operative has been posted here to Terminus. It could mean that someone here in Service headquarters suspects something."

A silence. "Well, what if he finds Ymaal?"

"See to it he does not."

"Easier said than done. I said he looked soft, not stupid."

"Lay down a false trail. Lead him in circles. He will tire after a while of fruitless search and perhaps head off in the direction of the Others. Sooner or later it will occur to him or Urmaal to investigate the strange 'accidental' death of Doctor Frryml more thoroughly."

Stubbornly. "And if he won't be led in circles? He looks a hunter. What if he picks up the spoor?"

A deep sigh of frustration. "We'll deal with that when we come to it. Just remember that there are two ways to solve the problem of Krral and Ymaal meeting. In any case, the Lefthand Pathway must be protected at all costs. If all else fails, perhaps we'll have to turn to the Eyes yet again. But let us hope not. Peace through transcendence."

"I understand. Liberation from the Paradox."

"Urmaal has what?"

"She has obtained detailed information on the wounds of all those who have committed suicide in the last five years."

"But that data was . . ."

"She is very persistent. She found a way around all our blocks. This could be serious."

A considering pause. "I think not. All she will discover is that the wounds were all delivered by the same kind of knife. What of it?"

"It was the same kind of knife that delivered the wound which killed Doctor Fymaal."

"Ah. Then they did do it. The fools! The Faction is proving to be almost as troublesome as the Deluded Ones or Urmaal!"

A shrug. "Perhaps we should use them to take care of our problem with Urmaal." Hastily. "I'm not suggesting I agree with their viewpoint that murder is as ultimate an experience as death! Merely that they might prove a useful tool in this case.''

"Tools like the Faction have a nasty habit of turning in the hand and cutting those who use them. I would rather send them all to Solution than use them or their cursed insanity in any fashion! They are murderers and nothing more!''

A tense pause. Then a sigh. "So. Now of Krral? He has gone to Ranth-urrl-Gobnar to search for that attendant?''

"Fmaal. Yes. He is there now. We have traced him as far as a place called Terminus.''

"Ha! How appropriate! Terminus. Yes, indeed. And what do you suppose will happen to him?''

A shrug. "The odds are good Terminus will prove his terminus, as you cleverly hinted just now. The Deluded Ones will not be pleased to have him sniffing around. I suspect that even now they are plotting his death.''

"Good. Let the blood be on their claws. Very well. Peace and endless sleep.''

"Endless sleep without dreams.''

*Shall any gazer see with mortal eyes,*
*or any searcher know by mortal mind?*
*Veil after veil will lift—*
*but there must be*
*veil upon veil behind.*

Sir Edwin Arnold
The Light of Asia

The Ranthaa who was in charge of Records at the medical center had obviously been there forever. Though she claimed to know nothing of any Ymaal or Fmaal, and proved it by letting him access files on her own keypad, when he showed her the picture of Ymaal/Fmaal, her eyes dilated just slightly in recognition. "No," she said very firmly, handing him back the picture, "never laid eyes on that particular Ranthaa. You must have the wrong medical center, friend. Your classmate never served here."

Krral sighed deeply. As he reached out to take the picture, he missed it and it fell to the floor next to her desk. He leaned over swiftly and retrieved it. For the instant he was down, his hand moved under the bottom edge of her desk and deposited a small round disk there. He straightened almost instantly with the picture in his hand and an apologetic grin on his face. "Sorry. Always been a bit clumsy. Sure is strange you don't recognize her, because I'm sure she's from around here. I must have seen her certificate a hundred times and I know it said that she served at the center in Terminus." He shrugged. "Oh, well, maybe I'll just ask around some more. Maybe somebody will remember her. Though it sure is odd about the lack of a file. Sure is."

He rose and left the office. Just down the hall was a bathroom. He entered and found it empty. Quickly he pulled out the tiny receiver he carried on his harness disguised as a medallion. He held it up to his ear to listen.

The conversation was already in progress. "... knows both her real name and her alias. I tell you, he's from Tech like I'm from Food. He's a Service operative, just like the last one."

"Did you give him any information?"

"Nothing. All the files are erased. I saw to that after the last one got so snoopy. That won't happen again. But you better warn her anyway. Tell her to stay out there and not come near the center or anything else in Terminus."

There was a pause. "I don't know. She's awfully jumpy as it is, you know. If she finds out there's a Service operative looking for her, she just might panic. But staying away from Terminus is a good idea. I'll tell her that."

"Good. Look, he's stalking around the center right now asking about her. I'm going to call a few who know to warn them. Especially Nurrl. I don't want that fool to spill anything by chance."

"Good idea. Go do it. See you."

The connection broke off just as a Ranthrr came into the bathroom. Krral casually put the medallion back on his harness, adjusting its position as if that had been his intention. He nodded at the Ranthrr and noticed that his name badge said Nurrl. *Now isn't that an interesting coincidence*, Seeker commented. *Terminus just seems to be filled with coincidences.*

*Dumb luck, I call it*, Krral replied with a mental shrug.

*Huh*, Seeker snorted. *I've always found that coincidences are really nothing but events you don't yet know the reasons for. And we Questioners always try to be extra cautious about things when we don't know the reasons for them. It's one of the first lessons you learn on Labyrinth.*

*Sensible*, Krral commented. *But I see no sense in wasting an opportunity even if it's put in your path. One never knows what one will learn. Think I'll switch tactics from sweetness and light to something more natural to me.*

Before the other Ranthrr knew what was happening, he was up against the wall with Krral's claws touching his nose. "One sound out of line," Krral growled menacingly, "so much as a soft purr, and your face is minus a muzzle." Nurrl nodded silently, his eyes wide with fear and shock.

Krral took the picture of Ymaal/Fmaal from the pouch on his harness and held it up before Nurrl's frightened eyes. "You know her. She used to work here. Seen her lately?"

Nurrl paused and Krral brought his claws to the tip of the other Ranthrr's nose. Nurrl swallowed and nodded ever so slightly. " 'Bout a week ago," he murmured weakly, his voice quavering just slightly. "She . . . stopped by to talk with Raaml in Records. Old friends."

"Where is she now?"

Nurrl closed his eyes and whined slightly. "Don't know. Out someplace. Not in Terminus."

"Where's 'out someplace'? Come on, Nurrl. My patience is wearing thin. Spill it."

"I don't know. Really I don't. They all hang out there. Out there somewhere."

"They all? Who's they all?"

Nurrl's whine had become a whimper. "I can't say. I don't dare. Leave me alone. Go out there yourself and see. I can't say any more or they'll . . .' "

Krral sheathed his claws and smashed his fist into the side of Nurrl's head. The Ranthrr collapsed in a heap. "Oooooopppsss, sorry," Krral said sarcastically to the unconscious body. "I'm kind of clumsy, you know." He stepped quickly to the door, opened it and looked both ways. The corridor was empty. He calmly stepped out, went down the corridor to the main hallway and then left the center.

"This is getting interesting," Krral muttered under his breath as he walked back to his lodgings. "We know she's here, Questioner."

"Not here, but 'out there.' With 'them,' perhaps. The question now is where is 'out there' and who is 'them'? Maybe we should take Trrulul up on his offer of a drink. If anybody knows where 'out there' is, he should."

"Agreed. But I don't trust that particular Ranthrr any further than I can throw him. And he's big enough that throwing him would be a hefty task. We're getting closer to the quarry, Questioner. And the hunt is always most dangerous then."

"Then we must both be extra alert," Seeker replied.

Krral nodded and fell silent.

\* \* \*

" 'Out there?' " Trrulul slurred. "Where'd you ever hear that phrase?"

"Somebody mentioned it," Krral responded vaguely, his voice blurred with drink. He was anything but drunk. He had taken two anti-intoxicant pills before entering the drinking den with Trrulul and his two miner friends. "Sounded interesting. 'Out there.' Nice ring to it." He burped.

"Nice ring to it! Ha! Tha's a good one! By my next nexus, tha's a good one! 'Out there,' my friend from Ranthar, refers to the surface. To death! To the sandy wastes of Gobnar! The only ring to that is the ring of a Ranth's dying roar."

"Can anybody live out there?" Krral asked innocently.

"Sure. For months. If you know exactly what you're doing," one of the other miners offered. Trrulul glared at him and he shut up.

"Really? How? Thought you could only last days."

"It's in the caves you can survive," Trrulul stated. "Terminus caves open onto the surface. Only a small opening, and it's protected with a lock. But it's in a mountain of solid bedrock. Not many mountains on Gobnar. Wind and sand scour them right down to nubbins. But this here mountain is volcanic glass. Lots of bubble caves in it. Some even have water. Sure you can survive out there for months. If you know exactly what you're doing. And if you're damn lucky."

"Why lucky?"

Trrulul snorted. "Cause 'pedes like caves like that. And 'pedes like water too. And where there's 'pedes, that's where you don't want to be, friend. Ha! No degree from Tech will help you then! What'd you say your degree was in?"

"Didn't. But it was in engineering. Worked with molecular disrupters. You know, for mining."

The miners grunted acceptance. Krral was very glad he'd studied the background Urmaal had provided for his alias. One of the miners raised dim eyes to Krral's. "You want to go out there, friend? Only one reason to go out there. Tha's Eyes. Tha's where the Eyes are. You come here to hunt Eyes?"

They were all watching him intently. He hesitated before answering. "Well . . . not exactly. I mean, I remember my friend Ymaal mentioning something about it, but she's why I came, not Eyes." They all relaxed slightly. "But . . . since she doesn't seem to be here, maybe . . ."

Trrulul chuckled. "Oh, you're a sharp one, you are! If you can't find your sweet little Ranthaa, you'll settle for Eyes! Ha! Ha! And just maybe you might have beginner's luck, eh, boys? Maybe we should go out with him and see if he does, eh?"

The other growled slight agreement. Krral looked woozily around at them. "How 'bout just showin' me where 'out there' is? I don't know if I'm really up to actually goin' out on the surface of anything as dangerous as Gobnar. But I guess I'd like to at least *look* out."

"Ha! Ha!" Trrulul roared with laughter. "So's you can have a story to tell 'em back on Ranthar, eh? Why, sure, friend. Nothing's easier. Be glad to show you the lock to the outside. Even take you out for a quick look-see. Why not, eh, boys?" They all mumbled agreement. "Then let's go," Trrulul bellowed as he rose, weaving, to his feet. "All together! To give our friend from paradise a glimpse of hell!"

# II.

They took a small electric cart through the winding caverns, slowly leaving the more settled parts behind. As they trundled into the uninhabited sections of the cavern, Trrulul turned on the cart's lights, for the illumination which filled the areas where Ranth lived was more sparsely placed in the unused portions. Eventually it ceased altogether and they had to depend solely on the illumination provided by the cart. For most of the journey, there was no discernible upgrade. Near the end, however, in rugged, narrow tunnels, the rise was more sudden and easily noticed.

They reached a point where the cart could no longer handle the grade or the roughness of the tunnel floor. For perhaps another mile, guided by the lights the miners carried attached to their harnesses, they walked through the increasingly narrow and rugged tunnel until they came to a wider space. The space had been cut from the rock and contained several large cabinets in which hung protective suits, breather packs and other equipment. On one wall there was a datanet terminal with information flashing on its screen. At the far end of the space was a door that reminded Krral of the airlocks on space ships. He felt sure it was the way to the surface.

Trrulul went over to the datanet screen to check out the information. Laughing and grumbling among themselves, the miners helped Krral pick a suit and then get into it. They also fit him with a breather pack and made sure it was full. "Just remember," one of them leered drunkenly in Krral's face, "when you gets out there and gets scared, don't breathe too heavily or too fast like. This here breather only works if you breathes slow and easy like. In, out, in, out. Suck too hard and you gets nothing. Ha! Lots of first-timers passes out because they gets scared and breathes too deep and fast and gets no oxygen and boom! Down they goes! And then we gots to drag or carry 'em back in again! Ha! Ha! Or maybe just leave 'em out there for the 'pedes!" His foul breath almost made Krral gag, so the operative put the face mask up and started practicing his breathing.

When everyone was ready, Trrulul went to the door and fiddled with the knobs. Krral watched closely so he could do it himself if he wanted to go back out on the surface some time in the future. The burly miner spun the center wheel and the door sunk back with a heavy sigh. Beyond the door was an empty room exactly like the entry lock on a space craft. At its far end was a second door.

Trrulul paused at the second door and looked at the chronometer that was attached to his protective suit. "Datanet weather report says it's calm and no storms in the immediate area," he rumbled through his breather mask. "Early mornin' out there right now. Good time to go out. 'Pedes not really active 'til early evenin'. Course, the damn spiders are hunting, but they can't get through the suits. Walk lightly, stay together, and keep a sharp eye out." Krral noticed that all the miners had suddenly become sober. Clearly, that, if nothing else, indicated the actual degree of danger the surface represented. Krral resolved to be at his most alert. Trrulul stepped to the second door and opened it.

Ranth-urrl-Gobnar's sun had a bluish cast, so the dawn light that came slanting at them from the east as they emerged from the short tunnel that opened onto the surface was slightly purple. Krral paused and looked around. The view was stunning. They were about halfway up a slope of solid rock that continued up behind them for another three thousand feet. The rock had been carved into fantastic shapes by the blast of wind-driven sand. Bizarre forms twisted off in every direction, some vaguely animal-like in shape, others looking like strange, abstract sculptures. Krral had never seen anything like it in his life.

But it was the distance that was the most awesome. Beyond the mountain slope where they stood, space fell away toward the horizon in what looked at first glance like a heaving sea. Then one realized that the waves were standing still and were made of sand and gravel. But what sand and gravel! It came in all the colors of the rainbow! Reds and blues and greens and yellows. Here they were mixed to form a subtle beige filled with colors. There a stark yellow hill crested in green. Off and off the waves of color rolled, mixed and tinted by the sheer chance currents of the wind.

The wind was the next thing Krral noticed. It was blowing steadily, lifting small swirls of fine sand and sending them swishing across the landscape, chasing each other toward the endless horizon like playful, formless creatures.

Stark, empty, the surface of Gobnar was both oddly simple and yet incredibly complex. Krral wondered how anything could ever live on the face of this planet. Naturally, there would be arachnids. There were arachnids everywhere. But anything else, no matter how primitive, was amazing.

It was a harsh place, desolate and cruel. And yet it was beautiful. Though he was from a tropical world himself, Krral could feel the pull of Gobnar's severe beauty. It held a strange combination of deadly menace and peaceful transcendence. Normal worries and concerns simply evaporated in a place like this. One came face to face with the issue of existence in its most basic and naked form.

Krral turned to look at the others. They were standing as still as he was. Most were gazing out at their world. Trrulul was gazing at him. Krral nodded in recognition of Trrulul's attention. "It's . . . not what I expected," he quietly admitted to the miner.

Trrulul's expression softened for an instant. "Never is. Never is the same two times in a row. Last time I was out here"—he pointed to their left—"there was a blue mountain right over there, maybe two thousand feet tall. Now the blue is spread across the surface at random and the mountain is a valley. Sort of tells you something, eh?" He cocked his head to one side and gave Krral an appraising glance. "Not frightened, eh?"

"No," Krral replied slowly, thoughtfully. "Wary, yes. This

place clearly doesn't give you much margin for error. No second chances. But it also doesn't feel malevolent. Not like a Brranth or a Wrrn-tree. More indifferent than hostile, I guess. Above it all, not concerned positively or negatively with our lives or deaths. Place each foot with care, watch every grain of sand, keep your eye on the sky for weather change, and you might make it. But don't expect help.''

Trrulul growled appreciatively. "You've got it, Qurrl. That says it about as good as I've heard it said.'' He gestured widely at the face of Gobnar. "And it's beautiful, ain't it?''

"Yes," Krral replied softly, "it's beautiful. Can we walk around a bit?"

"Why not?" Trrulul chuckled. "Keep a sharp lookout for Eyes while you're at it, too. Never know. Just might stumble on one of 'em. Beginner's luck and all.'' Trrulul led the way down the slope. The other miners spread out in a line to search the ground.

About halfway down to the point where the sand dunes began, one of the miners to Krral's right called out, "Spiders!'' At the call, they all stopped and turned in his direction. He appeared to be looking about, peering at the ground. "Plants! Bugs!'' he finally called out. With a chorus of grunts, the miners all began to troop in his direction.

Not knowing what was going on, Krral joined them. One of the miners walking by his side said, "Where there's spiders, there's bugs. And where there's bugs there's plants.''

"So?" Krral asked.

The miner scratched his head through his protective suit. "Well, where there's plants, there's cracks. And sometimes, very rare sometimes, where there's cracks, there's Eyes.''

"Eyes and cracks come together? Odd. Why's that?"

"Nobody knows for sure. It's almost like they come squeezing up out of the cracks or something. Nobody knows. Haven't found all that many Eyes. Don't really understand what they are. Just that they come up where the cracks are and that those off-world traders will pay a bundle for them. Eerie is what I call 'em. Don't like 'em. But search for 'em all the same, 'cause if I find a nexus, well, I'm out of here, that's for sure.''

They arrived at the spot where the first miner had noticed the spiders. Krral looked down and could see the tiny creatures skittering across the ground in a frantic search for prey. Here and there, one of them had caught an insect and was sucking it dry. Krral also noticed that in some cases more than one spider seemed to have caught the prey, apparently working as a group, and all the hunters were sharing in the feast. He shuddered slightly. Arachnids were creepy enough. Social arachnids were just a bit too much. It was social arachnids that had developed sapience on a few worlds. He idly wondered if these were on their way to intelligence.

The miners searched the area thoroughly, but found nothing even resembling an Eye. When they finally were ready to quit, Trrulul reminded them all to check each other for hitchhiking spiders. "Don't want none of the damn things back in the caverns, so look sharp, all of you." None were found, so they trooped back to the lock once more. "Been out long enough," Trrulul grumbled. "Time we was getting back to workin' if it's our work shift, sleepin' if it's our sleep shift, or drinkin' if it's our rec shift! Can't spend all our time showin' newcomers the glories of Gobnar."

"Are there other caverns out here near the surface, Trrulul?" Krral asked. "You mentioned something about them once."

Trrulul gestured vaguely at the horizon. "Oh, they're here, all right. This mountain is lava and filled with gas-bubble chambers. Wind wears the lava away and the bubble becomes a cave. Find 'em all over the mountain. More on other mountains. Trouble with most of 'em is they aren't connected with anything down below. Take the ones around here, for example. Most just dead ends. The caverns that make up Terminus are all connected, so they're useful. These little caves on the surface ain't good for much but 'pede nests."

"So no one lives in them?"

"Nah. You can hide in them if a storm comes up. Provided the 'pedes haven't gotten there first. But no way to live in 'em. Usually no water in 'em. And they're too shallow." He gave Krral a sly look. "If you can't find your lady friend down below, this ain't no place to look. She lives out here, she's either a lot tougher than any of us, or she's just plain crazy. Either way, she wouldn't be the kind of gal for you, eh?"

Krral laughed. "No. I like 'em soft and fast!"

"Of course he was lying," Krral said. "Or at least he was only telling part of the story."

"You're probably right," Seeker replied thoughtfully. "I don't want to denigrate the danger of Gobnar's surface, but it doesn't seem all that much worse than other worlds I've experienced. With a proper shelter and caution, survival would be possible."

"More than possible," Krral rumbled. "Hard, but with the right cave and the right equipment, you could make it. I think that's one fact we can depend on. A second one is that I'll bet Ymaal is holed up in some cave out there right this very minute. The only problem is, where out there? From the look I got, the surface of Gobnar is pretty big."

"It seems most likely that she is not far from the opening to Terminus," Seeker suggested. "First, because she would need the proximity for supplies. Second, she is apparently involved with some group here. Remember the reference Nurrl made to 'them.' Therefore it seems likely she would want to be in contact with them."

"Hmmmmm. Seems likely. But from what Nurrl said, I got the distinct impression that 'they' were out there as well as in here. I wonder if Trrulul is one of 'them'?"

Seeker considered. "Not at all unlikely. There's one thing I'm a little hazy on, Krral. I can't seem to find any information on it in the data you've shared with me. What kind of groups are there among the Ranth that would be likely to be secret organizations involved with murder?"

Krral scratched his head. "That's a real cold trail, Questioner. I don't have any data to share with you because there isn't any, so far as I know."

"Odd. Are you saying that there aren't any dissident groups? Any discontented Ranth who would like to change things?"

"What would you change? Ranthar is paradise. Everyone has enough of everything. We only work to occupy our time and stimulate our minds. I could do anything, Questioner. I'm an operative with the Service because I find it fascinating. If I get tired of it, I'll just switch to something else. Nothing's simpler."

"But what about what Trrulul said about finding a nexus of Eyes so he'd have enough money to buy his way back from Gobnar to Ranthar? Surely, that sounds like discontent."

Krral nodded thoughtfully. "That was odd. Let me explain it to you and you'll see why it's so odd. All Ranth are born on Ranthar. We all spend a cubhood of about three years with our pride mother. Then we begin our cub training in the facilities provided by the pride's schools. Part of that takes place on the original plain where our species developed from the proto-Ranth, a species of social hunting felinoids.

"Cub training lasts about ten years. Then we go to school for ten more, studying something specific, like mining engineering. When our technical education is finished we're sent to one of the colony worlds to serve out the remainder of our First Hundred working in the mines, as on Gobnar, or in the jungle plantations, as I did on Urthar, or in some other task on one of the other worlds, or even on the terraforming projects on any of them. It's a hard period, one of challenge and trial. Some Ranth die. But more than ninety-five percent make it.

"For the Second Hundred, we usually come back to Ranthar itself, though some do choose to stay on their colony world and serve there as administrators and project directors. A few spend part of their Second Hundred on one world in one task, and then switch around later on. Urmaal did that. She spent the first part of her Second Hundred here, in fact.

"The Third Hundred is always the same. All Ranth come back to Ranthar. Many engage in the project that's looking for the answer to immortality. We're so close, Questioner!" His voice took on an edge of excitement. "We've been gaining on it every year! We could unlock the final secrets at any moment!"

"So I understand," Seeker said drily. "How many hundreds of years have you been on the brink of that discovery?"

Krral shrugged. "Many hundreds. We've followed a lot of dead ends. Met with many unexpected obstacles. But that's all past now. We know we're almost there this time. Think of it, Questioner! Living forever! We're already the longest-lived mammaloid species in the Federation. That's one of the reasons we've been able to accomplish so much. How much more can we do if we live forever? The possibilities are staggering! We'll literally become like gods!"

"I hate to change the subject," Seeker said ironically, "but we were talking of dissident groups."

"But that's the point! There's nothing to be dissident about! Every Ranth gets to Ranthar by their Second Hundred if they wish. Every Ranth has everything they want or need. Every

Ranth looks forward to imminent immortality. What Trrulul said is nonsense! You can't buy your way back to Ranthar. There's no reason to and no way. Everything is run by a process and everything is on the datanet. There's just no room for . . .'' Krral paused thoughtfully. ''And yet Ymaal's file was gone.''

''And people are committing suicide,'' Seeker reminded him softly. ''And Doctor Frryml was murdered. And you very nearly were. Not to mention me. Or your mate Mraal. And Bilrog.'' The Questioner paused. ''Krral, I hate to say this because I know it goes against everything you've ever learned, but this business about Ranthar being a paradise and every Ranth being a happy creature is full of holes. Something is drastically wrong here. And one of the most basic problems is that your attitude and beliefs about yourself and your race get in the way of your being able to see what it is that's wrong.

''I don't have your blind spots. That's the advantage Questioners have. We see things from an entirely different perspective. True, the only data I have right now is from your mind and tinged with your prejudices. But I'm slowly beginning to build up a picture of Ranth reality on my own. I admit it's far from complete yet. And I'm certainly not ready to make any judgements based on it. But even this early in the process, I can say one thing for sure. It doesn't necessarily match the one that's in your mind, Krral.''

The Ranthrr was silent for some time. When he finally spoke, his words were hesitant. ''I . . . think I understand. This isn't going to be . . . easy, Questioner. Maybe you're right. Maybe I just can't see things because I'm looking at them the wrong way. I was raised seeing things a certain way, the Ranth way. But . . . well, it's hard. We Ranth are so used to being superior and . . . to be so uncertain about the very things which make us superior . . . well, it may take me some time to adjust. But I'll work at it. Just give me a little time.''

''That's just the problem,'' Seeker said softly. ''You may not have much time left.''

''I think that's right,'' Krral said, his voice slightly muffled by the breather pack's mask.

''Yes. I paid close attention as well when the miners were adjusting the suit to fit you. You've done it right and the pack is full. Last time we were out about two hours and the pack still registered more than three-fourths full when you took it off. So I estimate that a pack will last at least eight to ten hours of continuous use.''

"I'm not sure continuous use is even necessary. I noticed several of the miners shifted to the other tube in the breather mask, the one that seems to connect to the outside air through that thing that looks like a filter on the left. Maybe if I switch back and forth every ten minutes or so, I could stretch the ten hours to fifteen or more. I really haven't the slightest idea how long this will take and I'd like to leave as much leeway as possible.''

Seeker agreed and Krral spun the center wheel of the second door. The door sighed open and they stepped through into the short cave that opened onto the surface.

Once they were in the open, Krral looked around. As with the last time they were out, the sky was cloudless. "Not enough free water in the atmosphere to form clouds," Seeker suggested. "Makes it hard to tell if weather is coming.''

"Forecast on the datanet was good for the next twenty hours," Krral responded. "Wind will pick up a bit around the middle of the day." He paused. "Well, which way do we head? One seems as good as another to me.''

"Then," Seeker laughed, "it doesn't make any difference. How about toward the sun?''

Krral shrugged agreement and they set off.

An hour's walk in that direction discovered four shallow caves, all empty, and none really suitable for habitation by a Ranthar. In one of the caves, they found two 'pedes which Krral killed with well-placed stones. Other than that, the world seemed empty of life. There didn't even seem to be any spiders around.

As the sun climbed toward the zenith, Krral turned and headed back on a slightly different path. Again, they found nothing more interesting than a few small pockmarks in the hard, volcanic rock of the mountain.

They made another sweep toward the north with similar results. It wasn't until they walked westward that things became more interesting.

It was the middle of the afternoon when they found the first cave of any size. Krral crouched warily at the opening, which was about four feet high, and peered in, shining his light into the blackness. The cave was about ten feet deep and low. There was no sign of water or of any habitation by any living creature. Despite that, Krral felt elated. "We're getting closer," he told Seeker. "I can feel it."

About two hours later they found a major cave. The opening was only about four feet across, but it rapidly expanded past that to form a tunnel that even Krral could stand comfortably in. They stood tensely, listening and testing the air. "I would swear there's a touch of moisture in the air," Krral murmured. "We may have found something, Questioner."

"The question is," Seeker replied, "whether we follow it up now or come back some other time. We've been out looking around now for about seven hours. It's about an hour back to the entrance to Terminus."

Krral considered. "I vote we explore this cave a bit. Say for half an hour. Then if nothing comes of it, we make a quick search of the immediate area to see if there are any others like it. If we find some, or if not, we head back to the entrance and call it a day. Sound good to you?" Seeker agreed, so they went cautiously forward into the tunnel.

After about twenty feet, the tunnel twisted sharply to the right, then to the left. At that point, it narrowed and shrunk down so that it was necessary to stoop almost double to proceed. Crawling on his hands and knees, Krral shone his light ahead and suddenly stopped. "Fresh spoor," he muttered. "Look." He pointed to what appeared to be a dark cloth that blocked the passage. It hung from ceiling to floor of the tunnel. "A barrier to hold in moisture and oxygen. I think we may have found what we're looking for."

Seeker agreed. "Likely. Which means that things are becoming very dangerous. Hunt lightly, as Ranth say. Let's both be as alert as possible."

Carefully, Krral pushed back the hanging cloth. There was another piece just beyond it. He lifted that and crept forward, shining his light on the ground in front of him, moving with all the stealth he was capable of.

Within a few feet, the tunnel rose again and Krral was able to stand normally. It also became wider. Softly, as if stalking the most dangerous of game, Krral moved forward, placing each foot gently, precisely, every sense tuned to its highest pitch.

Unexpectedly, the walls of the tunnel fell back and they found themselves in a small chamber perhaps twenty feet across. It contained several protective suits hanging on one wall along with their breather packs. Krral shone his light on them. "We found it!" he hissed exultantly. "This must be the 'out there' where 'they' are that Nurrl blabbed about. Ymaal must be here!"

*Krral!* Seeker warned silently. *Unless your senses are deceiving me, someone is coming from that tunnel on the right!*

Krral turned swiftly and crouched down, dousing his light. For several seconds he remained motionless, listening and staring into the dark. There was nothing to be seen or heard and yet he knew Seeker was right. Someone or something was coming through the darkness of that tunnel toward the chamber. *Too late to retreat,* he said silently to Seeker. *We'll have to fight.*

There was a slight rustle to his left. Krral strained his eyes, trying to pierce the stygian blackness. A sigh from the left. 'Pedes? Or something worse? Should he turn his light on so he could at least see to fight? Or would that simply make him an easier target?

Without warning, lights went on and Krral was momentarily blinded. "It's that damn Qurrl," he heard a familiar voice growl out. "Only I've got a feeling he ain't named Qurrl and he ain't from Tech!"

As Krral's sight returned, he could see there were four of them. One was Trrulul in his miner's clothes. The other three were strangely clad in black cowled robes that hung loosely almost to the floor. They seemed to be made of some light material that flowed fluidly as those who wore them moved. Krral could not make out the features hidden within the hoods, but by their general shape he knew they were Ranthrr. "Hello, Trrulul," he said softly, still in his crouch. His claws were fully out and he watched the four Ranthrr for the slightest hostile move. "Surprise meeting you here where you said no one lived."

Trrulul growled deeply. He was standing tensely, in fighting stance, his shoulders hunched and his claws out. "Surprise ain't half of it, friend. You're in deep trouble. You can come with us nice and quietly, or we will carry you, hopefully not too badly injured. What's it gonna be, eh?"

Krral straightened slowly. He looked from one silent form to the other. Three he might have taken. But the fourth one was more than he cared to try, especially when he knew so little. It was time to wait and see. He sheathed his claws and shrugged. "I'm no fool. I'll come quietly."

"Wise choice," Trrulul answered with evident relief in his voice. He stood straighter and pulled his own claws in. "Follow me and don't try anything stupid if you want to live very long. Believe me, evening is coming and we know exactly where the 'pedes have their nests. Unless you want to end up feeding their young, just do as you're told, eh?" He turned and headed toward the tunnel, gesturing for Krral to follow. The other three fell in silently behind the operative. *Well,* he commented wryly to Seeker, *I imagine we'll get to see Ymaal, at least. I just hope she isn't the last thing we see.*

*If they had wanted to kill you, they could have done so very easily in the dark,* Seeker said. *Since they didn't, I assume they don't want you dead just yet. Which probably means they want to know more about why you are here, who you are, what you already know, and who else knows it. The problem is that if you tell them what they want to know, they may feel safe to kill you. And if you don't tell them, they may feel compelled to kill you.*

*Very logical,* Krral commented drily. *Never realized before how much I hate logic that makes me the kill no matter how it's figured. Nothing to do but wait and see.*

The five of them continued down the tunnel for perhaps two hundred feet. Then a small tunnel opened off toward the left and they took it. Another two hundred feet and the tunnel widened into a chamber about fifteen feet across, with two other openings, both covered with black cloth. They stopped in the center of the chamber and one of the Ranthrr in the black robes gestured to Krral to sit on the floor. Then the black-clad Ranthrr pushed aside the covering of the righthand opening and stepped through.

Krral estimated he sat there on the floor for no more than fifteen minutes before the Ranthrr returned, another Ranthrr following him. This second Ranthrr made Krral stare. It was very old, its pelt a silvery white in color, its eyes a weak, watery blue. But there was a bright light shining deep within them. And the Ranthrr turned that light directly and frankly on Krral.

As Krral stared at the newcomer, who was probably the oldest Ranthrr he had ever seen, he felt a growing sense of discomfort and dismay. This creature, he realized, had a strange power in its glance, a power which compelled and commanded. It was obvious the others in the chamber held it in highest esteem.

For several moments he met its glance. Then something within him quailed and he dropped his eyes. It was the first time in his life such a thing had ever happened. He felt slightly humiliated.

The ancient Ranthrr chuckled quietly. "So this is Qurrl. Or should I say, Krral?" He chuckled again. "Yes, Krral it is. Let us have only the truth between us, eh? I've heard much of you, Krral. Some of the others said you'd never find this place, never trace Ymaal here. But I knew better. I knew that you are truly a hunting Ranth of the old style. There is a fierceness in you that speaks of blazing sun and open veldt, of flashing claws and blood-drenched teeth, of head thrown back in a killing roar." He chuckled a third time. "Trrulul, you are lucky Krral decided to come peacefully. I wager he would have struck at you first. And if he had, I suspect you would have transcended the Paradox by now."

Krral lifted his eyes to meet those of the ancient Ranthrr. He grinned slightly, showing his teeth. "You are right, old one. And who might I have the honor of addressing?"

"I am called Master Grrul by most of those who know of me. But that seems rather formal for a hunting Ranth. Grrul will be enough between the two of us."

"And Ymaal is here." It was a statement, not a question.

"Indeed she is. She has asked me to ask you to forgive her for what she almost did. She knows it was wrong and is profoundly sorry. But sometimes one has duties to a higher authority and, well . . ." He shrugged slightly. "I'm sure you understand."

"I'd like to talk to her, question her."

Grrul sighed sadly. "I'm afraid that won't be possible. She has decided to enter the Order of Silent Preparation and has taken an oath of silence. She now dwells all alone in a small cave far, far out in the desert. There she will remain, in deep meditation and thought until she achieves her own transcendence. It was always her fondest wish, her real vocation. But she proved so useful to us in other ways that we refused her the right to it for many years. Now we can no longer deny the right. And besides, her value on Ranthar is dubious at best at this point.''

''She's dead,'' Krral declared flatly.

''Hardly,'' Grrul replied. ''She is very much alive. But in ways you would not really understand, Krral. She has met the Paradox face to face, has stood at the Crossroads Where Thought Hesitates, and has chosen the Lefthand Pathway. Now, at last, she walks that Pathway.''

''You're talking rubbish,'' Krral growled. ''Listen, Grrul, that little bitch tried to murder me. And I more than half suspect she may have been involved in the murder of my mate. There are things she knows that . . .''

Grrul held up a grizzled hand. ''Ymaal is guiltless in the case of Mraal. And she is too young to have been involved with what happened to Snurrl. That was long ago when things were very different in the Lefthand Pathway.'' He sighed deeply. ''We have learned much since then. Snurrl would not die now. There are other ways.''

He paused and stared morosely at Krral. ''Other ways,'' he repeated in a murmur. ''I almost wish they were not necessary in your case, Krral. I would really rather you carry a message back to Urmaal about Snurrl to tell her that her Blood Right is almost complete. She rid the universe of the direct actors. And time will soon rid it of the last indirect actor. The others are already gone and only I remain. She will outlive me and so triumph in her own narrow way.''

Grrul paused. Suddenly the strange light in his eyes blazed forth. ''But her way is so narrow! She sees not the possibilities! She has not faced the Paradox and made the choice! I will die, but only in this earthly sense, the sense of the Paradox! For I shall transcend and go beyond that point of the Crossroads! Beyond the death that seems the only way out of the Paradox!''

Krral stared in awe at the glowing, transformed face of Master Grrul. For several moments, the ancient Ranthrr seemed no longer of this world. He was rather a creature from some unimaginable otherwhere, a transcendent being that had somehow stepped over the boundaries of here and now and was mostly dwelling in another realm.

Krral shook his head to clear it. "Why can't I take your message back to Urmaal? What 'other ways' are you talking about? Why all this mystery?"

Grrul's gaze became earthly once more, pulled back from those rarer realms by a heavy burden of sorrow. "I would not kill you, Krral, though there are those of my followers who counsel such. They would feed you to the 'pedes." He shook his head sadly. "Forgive them, for they do not yet understand, they have not yet walked far enough on the Pathway.

"No. I would not kill you. Killing is the way of those caught in the Paradox and I would have none of it any longer. I regret any killings that have ever been committed in the name of the Lefthand Pathway and will allow no more.

"But at the same time, we cannot permit you to return to Ranthar with all you know. And then, of course, there is the matter of the Questioner." He peered intently at Krral. "I can see nothing that would indicate you carry one, but then I've never met anyone who has. Since I cannot see or sense the presence of the Questioner, I will merely ask it to pardon us for what must be done to protect the Lefthand Pathway. I'm sure it will understand. I also want it to know that we are not guilty of the death of Mraal and whatever happened to the Questioner she was host to.

"But back to you, Krral. We cannot let you return to Urmaal with what you know. She is still bent on her revenge, her Blood Right for Snurrl. If she knew where we were, untold disaster could happen to many innocent people. You have no idea how insane she is on this issue. For years now she has hounded us, seeking us out. We have done our best to avoid her. It has cost several lives.

"We will not add yours to that number. No more. But we will have to do something to you, something that will make you, ummmm . . . forget what you have learned. Yes. We will have to do something to your mind, I fear. But you will survive and they will care for you very well back on Ranthar. I understand there are wonderful facilities for Ranth who lose their minds. Yes."

Grrul stopped and stared solemnly at Krral. "It is regrettable, to be sure. But the Lefthand Pathway must be protected at all

costs. I am deeply and truly sorry.'' His gaze shifted to Trrulul.
''Take him to the Cave of the Eyes. Leave him there until
tomorrow. Then you will return his body to Terminus. Only
the Gods know where his mind will be.''

# III.

❧❦❧

*It was then the fear began.*
*And with the fear came serious reflection.*
                    Albert Camus
                    The Plague

Trrulul led the way again, muttering beneath his breath. The other three followed in total silence. Krral was as silent as they, and within his mind, Seeker was still as well. They moved swiftly along a constantly narrowing tunnel that slanted sharply upward.

Eventually, the muttering leader held up a hand to halt them. He turned to face Krral, a deep scowl on his face. Wordlessly he pointed to a small opening near the bottom of the left wall of the tunnel. "In there. Crawl in about five feet. Then you'll be able to stand." He dropped his eyes to gaze fixedly at the floor.

"Any light? Or do I just stand in the dark?" Krral asked.

"Oh, there's light. Mor'n you'll want, believe me. You'll have no trouble seein' at all." Trrulul suddenly raised his eyes and stared fiercely into Krral's face. "I'd not do it this way, not at all. I'd give you a clean death, a hunter's death. But he's got funny ideas." He gestured with his head back to where they had left Master Grrul. "He's a deep one and I don't understand him at all. I just do what he says, 'cause he's the Master. But I don't have to like it all the time. Not at all. Now in with you."

Krral knelt and crawled slowly into the opening. As Trrulul had said, the tiny tunnel went in for about five feet and then expanded so that even a full grown Ranthrr could stand comfortably. And it wasn't dark. From up ahead a strange, bluish glow filled the air. Curious, Krral moved forward toward it.

The new tunnel he was in made a sharp turn to the left, then to the right. With each step the light became brighter. Suddenly the tunnel turned sharply left and opened into a large cavern, perhaps fifty feet across by thirty wide. The ceiling rose a good thirty feet above him. The blue light that bathed the whole cavern and leaked into the tunnel seemed to come from the very walls themselves. It filled the space completely and made everything in the cavern clearly visible. The odd thing was that there were no shadows. Even Krral himself didn't cast one.

Everywhere Krral looked, there were piles of small round objects that looked very much like smooth white pebbles. Many more were stuck on the walls as if they were in the process of oozing out of the rock. Krral walked several paces into the cavern, looking around in wonder. He looked more closely at one of the pebbles that happened to be at the top of a pile of perhaps fifty others. It was approximately two inches in diameter and appeared almost perfectly spherical. It seemed to glow dimly on its own, a soft light coming from inside as though it was slightly translucent and a blue candle burned in its depths. He stared hard at it.

And suddenly it was staring back.

Krral jerked his head back in astonishment. The other pebbles in the piles turned into staring eyes. It was sudden and utterly unexpected. One moment the pebbles were glowing, whitish things. The next they were staring eyes.

"Eyes!" Krral murmured in wonder. "A whole cavern full of them! If a few of them are so valuable, this place must be . . . must be . . ." He stopped because he simply couldn't find the words. And also because the other pebbles in the cavern, the thousands and thousands of them, were swiftly opening and staring at him.

The impact was incredible and staggered his mind. He straightened into a rigid posture and looked wildly around the cavern. "They're all glaring at me, Questioner. What in the world are they?"

"I suspect you're right and that they are the Eyes we've heard so much about. Perhaps this is where they are 'born,' so to speak. And then they must work their way out to the surface. Very odd. It's almost as if . . . as if they were alive."

"Alive?" Krral echoed hollowly. "Yes, yes, they seem alive. That's what she said, you know, that they seem alive. Creepy, too." He growled deep in his throat. "Creepy. By my pride, Questioner! There are thousands of them just staring at me! What do they want?"

There was a slight note of hysteria in Krral's tone that surprised Seeker. "Want? Nothing, I imagine. They must react to the presence of life by opening that way. Could you pick one up? I'd like to examine it more closely."

"Pick one up?" Panic resonated in Krral's voice. "Touch one of them? Touch a staring Eye? So many of them! What do they want? Why are they staring at me like that?"

Seeker realized that something was very wrong. "Krral, get hold of yourself! There's no need to be frightened until we know more. These things are probably totally harmless . . ."

"Harmless?" he hissed in dread. "No. See them? They're staring at me! Staring the way a predator stares at its prey! Staring, glaring, unblinking eyes boring into me, peering at me, looking for . . . looking for the weak spots . . . the . . ."

"Snap out of it!" Seeker shouted. "By my six pouches, there's nothing to be afraid of! Krral, stop it!"

Krral buried his head in his hands, covering his eyes. His whole body was shaking violently. "Can't," he moaned hoarsely. "Damn things. Staring at me. Can't even shut them out. It's no use. They can see me even when I'm hiding. No place to run. Too many of them. Questioner! Save yourself! I . . . I . . ."

It was clear to Seeker that something about the thousands of staring Eyes was profoundly affecting Krral's mental stability. Quite literally, the Ranthrr was coming apart at the seams. At the same time, the Eyes had absolutely no effect on the ursoid, unless piquing its curiosity counted. But Krral was the host, and if the host went mad, then Seeker would find itself in a mind where its own existence would be dangerously threatened. There was only one thing to do and Seeker did it.

Seeker took control. Gently, but firmly, the Questioner pushed Krral into a quiet corner of his own mind, isolating him from external contact. When Seeker had completed the task of settling his host and calming him down, it picked up one of the Eyes and studied the strange object with fascination.

Was it alive? Or was it something that transcended the boundary of live/dead matter and created a new category all its own? No one had ever been able to determine exactly where the line between mere chemical complexity and true life began. Seeker wondered if the thing it was holding in its hand was something unique, something which spanned both categories. It was warm to the touch, yet hard and solid like a rock. Seeker extended one of Krral's claws and tried to scratch it. No effect. Then the Questioner dropped it. Again, no effect. And yet it does seem to *look* at me, Seeker decided.

Seeker wandered around the cavern. All over the walls were new Eyes emerging from the rock. The rock itself, the ursoid noticed, was not the same as the volcanic material which made up the rest of the complex of tunnels and caverns it had been in. This seemed radically different, softer, almost porous, and definitely glowing with its own inner luminescence.

Finally, having done all the exploring it could, the Questioner returned to the center of the Cave of the Eyes and simply sat and waited for Trrulul to come back. It made gentle contact with its host to see how he was doing. Krral was resting fitfully in his corner of the mind they shared. The Ranthrr had been badly shaken by his experience, but was rapidly recovering his equilibrium. He felt rather sheepish about his instability and assured Seeker it had been totally unexpected. Seeker could feel the anger and hard resolve that was building in the Ranthrr.

It was one of the hooded figures that came into the cavern to get Krral, its cowl pulled well forward to shield its view of the Eyes. Holding Krral by the hand as if he were a small and frightened cub, the other Ranthrr guided him out into the main tunnel again. Trrulul and one other were waiting.

*I'll take over again now, Questioner,* Krral stated flatly. With a mental nod, Seeker stood aside and gave the Ranthrr full control of his mind and body.

Trrulul was standing in the middle of the tunnel, directly in front of Krral. The hooded Ranthrr that had come to get him was by his left side. The other hooded figure stood slightly to Trrulul's left and behind him.

Krral's left hand came slamming up and delivered a stunning back-fisted blow to the muzzle of the Ranthrr by his side. Then Krral's foot shot out and caught Trrulul right in the lower stomach. Stepping forward with the kick, Krral aimed his right hand at the head of the third Ranthrr and knocked it sprawling. It hit the wall with a thud, its head ramming into the solid rock with dangerous force. Unconscious, it slid down to the floor and lay in a crumpled heap. The first one was already staggering to its feet, blood pouring down its face. Krral kicked it in the side of the head and it fell heavily to the ground. Trrulul was bent over, gagging and trying to catch his breath. Krral grabbed the front of his harness and hauled him upright, at the same time slamming him backward against the opposite wall of the tunnel. The miner tried to struggle and Krral slapped him hard in the face. With a whimper, Trrulul subsided and stared at Krral with frightened eyes.

"You . . . you're supposed to be . . ."

"Yeh. But I'm not." Krral flicked out his claws. "Note these claws, friend. They're specially shaped and they're damn sharp. Sharp enough to rip the side of your face off with one swipe. Which is something I'd dearly love to do. Now you do what I say, and you do it fast, or I'll leave your face splattered all over these walls. Understand?"

Trrulul whimpered slightly and nodded.

"The task is simple enough even for a fool like you, Trrulul. Just take me to Master Grrul. Think you can handle that? Or do I dismantle your good looks?"

"I . . . I'll take you. That's what I came for. To get you and bring you back to him. He wanted . . . wanted to see . . ."

"To see if I was crazy enough to send back to Terminus. Well, I'm not. So let's go. And don't try any tricks. I'm about twice as fast as you are and about as soft as these volcanic rocks. And I'd really like an excuse to bust you up some. Move it, Trrulul!"

Walking as though he expected to be struck dead at any moment, the miner took Krral back down the tunnel and to a small chamber Krral had not been in before. There, seated calmly in its center, was Master Grrul.

As they stepped in, Master Grrul looked up. His eyes widened in surprise as he understood the situation. Then a frown of concern wrinkled his brow. "The other two? I hope they aren't badly hurt."

"They'll need something for their headaches, but they'll survive. I'm not sure I can say the same about you, though.

It'll all depend on the little talk we're about to have." Krral growled menacingly. "Don't bother to call for any help. It'd never get here in time."

Master Grrul smiled slightly. "I wasn't even thinking of it. As you noticed, there aren't any guards in the tunnels or at my door. We don't need guards here. We are all one in the Lefthand Pathway and such things are not required."

The old Ranthrr paused and gazed at Krral. "May I say that I am truly surprised to see you in this . . . condition. The Eyes generally have a rather . . . different effect."

"Credit given where credit due. You tell him, Questioner."

"Hello, Master Grrul," Seeker said. "The Eyes would have driven Krral insane. But they had virtually no effect on my mind. So I took over for a while. Nothing simpler."

Master Grrul was staring in utter fascination at Krral. "Amazing," he murmured. "When the Questioner is there, it is still Krral, but not Krral." He sat back and nodded. "Such a thing has never happened. But now it has and so it must have been meant to be. Krral has been saved for reasons and purposes I cannot hope to fathom. But so be it. I shall not interfere."

"How about some answers?" Krral growled. "I'm going to get them one way or another. And believe me, it's better for all concerned if I don't have to ask twice."

Master Grrul laughed. "I hardly intend to resist, my fierce hunting Ranthrr! Ask away! If the answer is mine to give, it will be a pleasure to give it."

"Where is Ymaal?"

"Where none can reach her. She is deep in the desert in a cave, all alone, seeking Transcendence of the Paradox. Even I do not know where she is."

"That's not a very good answer."

"And yet it is the only one there is."

"Why did she try to kill me?"

The old Ranthrr sighed deeply. "That was a foolish mistake of someone who was too fervent in his attempts to protect the Lefthand Pathway. He has been properly punished. Such things will not be repeated."

Krral growled deeply. "What is your connection with Mrral's death, Grrul?"

Master Grrul paused and frowned. "That is hard to say. Directly, no connection whatsoever. But indirectly I fear we are somewhat culpable. You see, her investigations were coming very close to us and our people on Ranthar. So we planted some clues to divert her and put her on to the Others. It was after she began to investigate them that she was murdered. I suspect it was they who were directly involved."

Krral shook his head as if to clear it. "This is going around in circles. Every question uncovers more questions and every answer adds to the confusion. I hear you talking, Grrul, and even understand the words. But you don't seem to be getting anywhere. O.K. Who are the Others?"

"Ah, that is an even harder question. But I will do my best. They are the confused souls who have followed the logic unto death, but have followed it to the wrong conclusions. They have abandoned the Lefthand Pathway and travel on the Righthand Pathway. They merely change one death for another."

Krral gave Master Grrul a considering glance. "Make any sense to you, Questioner?"

"Something seems to be emerging. We're going down through layers and layers of meanings, trying to get to the kernel. May I take over for a few questions, Krral?"

"Be my guest," Krral rumbled.

Seeker paced back and forth for a few moments as it prepared its line of questioning. Master Grrul watched with fascinated eyes. Trrulul crouched a short distance away, looking very confused and frightened.

"Master Grrul," the Questioner finally said, "there's a word we've heard you use a couple of times recently. I wonder if you could explain it. What is the Paradox?"

The old Ranthrr sighed and sat back, looking very pleased. "So it is true. What they say of Questioners is true." He nodded slowly. "Yes, yes, you have gone to the heart of the matter with that question."

Master Grrul paused as if collecting his thoughts. When he began, his voice was soft and calm. "You may not understand all of this, Questioner, being an alien. But ask Krral for confirmation. I'm sure he will understand.

"We are a mighty race, one of the most favored in the galaxy. We live on many worlds and have control of them all. Our homeworld, Ranthar, is a paradise, as I am sure you have heard until you are sick of the hearing! We want for nothing. We live long lives, full lives, exciting lives. And just around the corner is the promise of immortality.''

Grrul paused and closed his eyes for a few moments. When he opened them again, they were filled with sadness. ''That is what we are taught from the time we are cubs. But let me tell you a slightly different tale.

''Once, many years ago, there was a young First Hundred Ranthrr on Ranth-urrl-Gobnar. He was very eager, very daring, a true hunting Ranth of the old style. And like the old Ranth, he had a life-mate, a Ranthaa he loved with all his heart and soul. They were inseparable and the only time they spent apart was when they were on different work details.

''One day the Ranthaa, let us call her Praal, was on the surface with a exploratory team. A sudden storm came up and the team scurried for what cover they could find. What they found was a fairly large and snug cave not far from here. It was a perfect refuge to hide in until the storm had passed.

''The storm blew through and the Ranthrr waited for his love to return. When the exploratory party failed to show up after two days, a search group was quickly organized and he led it out onto the surface of the planet. After two days of feverish searching, they found the cave, and the exploratory party.''

Grrul paused for several moments and stared off into empty space. His eyes were brimming with unshed tears. When he spoke again his voice was hoarse with emotion. ''Do you know about the centipedes, Questioner? In small groups of three or four, they are virtually harmless. But now and then, for breeding purposes, they come together in larger numbers, sometimes as many as four or five dozen. The males fertilize the females. Then there is a frenzy and they begin to attack each other. The weak are quickly immobilized by the poison in their bites. Immobilized, but not killed. They live in a state of suspended animation, breathing shallowly, alive, but barely. The surviving females then lay their eggs in these immobilized bodies. Hundreds of eggs. The eggs hatch and the larvae that come out of them eat their way into the bodies, slowly devouring them. Eventually they mature and within the remains of their feast, they turn to pupae. In a few days they hatch as tiny but perfectly formed centipedes. Hundreds of them come pouring out of the eaten carcasses. And once again they go into a frenzy, the stronger devouring the weaker until only a few dozen of the very most fit remain. Then the survivors, now almost fully grown, spread out over the surface of the planet.

"As I said, centipedes are not dangerous in small numbers to creatures as large as Ranth. But in large numbers they are deadly. They . . . will attack and bite and their jaws are strong enough to pierce even our protective suits. Enough bites and . . . and even a full-grown Ranth is paralyzed. Then the female centipedes . . . lay their eggs . . . in the Ranth . . . and . . ." His voice broke down and he was unable to continue. He sat for several moments breathing deeply to calm himself. Slowly his control came back.

"The eggs hatch very soon after being laid. And the larvae eat very swiftly into the bodies of their victims. Two, three days, and it is too late to do anything."

He paused again, considering, gazing at the air in a brooding manner. "We found them," he finally continued, his voice soft and wistful, "on the fifth day after the centipedes which had been hiding in the cave had attacked and paralyzed them. There was nothing to do but kill them. They were . . . still alive, you see, and very well aware of what was happening. The look in their eyes . . . the horror . . . and then the flash of . . . gratitude just before we killed them was . . ."

Grrul shook his head as if to dislodge something that was stuck there. "The whole search party made it back without further incident. But of the seven of us who made up the party, only three stayed on Gobnar. The others transferred off."

Seeker nodded. "Urmaal, Snurrl, and you stayed."

The old Ranth looked up sharply. "Yes. How did you know that, Questioner? There are only two Ranth alive who know that. Urmaal and I."

The Questioner shrugged. "Call it an informed guess. And a further guess tells me there's more to it than that. But I imagine we'll come back to it later."

Grrul nodded solemnly. "Yes. It fits better later on. The three of us were all changed by what had happened. For the first time we all realized something. Ranth can die. Ranth do die. All Ranth. And in the face of such a death as those Ranth met in the cave with the centipedes, what is the hope and glory of our race worth? Nothing. All our progress, our science, our damn paradise planet, it all avails nothing when death, especially a horrible death like that, stares you in the face.

"Why? Because all the glory is shared with others, all the hope of immortality, all the accomplishments. But our death, ah, our death cannot be shared. That is ours alone. All the pain, all the horror, all the despair, cannot be shared. It is ours, ours, ours. We are locked within it and cannot break out.

"But soon death will be no more, you say? Soon we will unlock the secrets of immortality and then all will be well. Rubbish. Some will still die as my mate died. It is inevitable. And what of all those who have died? What justice is there for them? They cannot live forever, for they are dead. How horrible to live eternally knowing you do so seated on the mounded dead of your ancestors!

"Soon, ah, so soon, we will open that last secret and be immortal at last. Rubbish once more. How long has that promise been held out to us? A thousand years now? At least. It has become an article of faith with Ranth everywhere. Just around the corner. Just beyond the next hill. Just the day after tomorrow. Hope. It is nothing but hope. And it is a hope based on an impossibility. It will never happen. Those in charge of the research know that. But they can't admit it even to themselves. It is a lie, a racial lie that keeps us going, going, going . . . toward what?"

Master Grrul paused and stared hard at Seeker. "That is the Paradox, Questioner. We hope, we believe, we will leave death behind. And in the midst of our hope, death comes to find us. In the face of such a thing our lives, our Three Hundreds are a bubble bursting, a foolish trifle, the blink of an eye. All eternity is death, and life but a fleeting instant.

"I said the three of us were changed by the experience. Urmaal and Snurrl turned inward toward each other and found what solace they could in each other's arms. I think . . . I went a little crazy after Praal died. I wandered through all the tunnels that extend far beyond Terminus, tunnels where no other Ranth has yet set foot. I wandered in the dark and the silence and it suited the darkness and silence of my own mind. Eventually I wandered out onto the surface. I lost my breather pack, my protective suit, yet somehow I survived. I must have learned to move more slowly, to accommodate myself to the lower oxygen content, to hide from the storms, find water, avoid the centipedes. I don't know. That whole time is wrapped in deep fog and no matter how hard I try, I cannot penetrate it.

"One day I awoke and found myself at the very top of the mountain beneath which we lie. I vaguely realized what had happened and the pain returned with renewed force. I found myself face to face with the Paradox in all its harsh brutality. And I decided then and there that I would not rest until I had either solved the Paradox or died in the attempt.

"I don't really know how long it had been since my last meal, but I felt no hunger. Except a burning hunger for release from the Paradox. So I found a niche hollowed out by the wind-driven sand and sat in it, facing east, determined to remain there until I had triumphed or died.

"All of that time is hazy and vague in my memory, like a vaguely remembered face in a fever dream. I moved in and out of consciousness. How long did I sit there? I have no idea. A day? A week? A year? A lifetime?

"All I do know for sure is that one morning, as the sun rose above the ever shifting landscape, the light broke over my mind and I understood! I saw the truth! Life, Questioner, *is* suffering and death. Or better yet, it is suffering that ends in death! Where does this suffering come from? It comes from our desire to live, from the desire for immortality, for happiness, for the things and emotions and loves and hates of life. Life generates desire in its search for some meaning beyond death, and these desires give us pain and suffering because they cannot be fulfilled in the face of inevitable death. Life is too fragile, too transitory to satisfy our desires and so we suffer ceaseless hunger and endless, futile hope. What is the answer? We must rid ourselves of our desires, of our hopes! Only by denying the very things life tries to make us affirm can we cease the suffering that makes life so unbearable.

"And my mind was overwhelmed with awe. For here was a second and greater Paradox behind the first! The first was the Paradox of Death in the midst of Life. The second was the Paradox of Life within Death. For I realized the only way to transcend the first Paradox was to give up the very nature of life itself. Only by giving up life and its suffering could we transcend death! Wonder of wonders! I rose from my place and with my heart singing, I came back once more into the caverns of the living Ranth."

"And that's what Ymaal is doing right now? She's out there

in a cave getting rid of her desires so she can transcend death?'' Seeker's tone was carefully neutral.

Grrul nodded. ''Yes. She must reject life in order to find it. When she has utterly rejected it, then no death can touch her. She will have transcended the Paradox.''

''How come you're not out there like her, Grrul?''

''Oh, you have no idea how I wish I could be! How I ache and yearn for the chance, Questioner! But when I came back among the Ranth again and began to tell my story, I realized I could not go back for a long time. I, and I alone, had walked the first portion of the Lefthand Pathway. I, and I alone, knew how to guide others to set their feet upon it. So I, and I alone, had to stay behind, even while they trod that path to transcendence, so that I might point the way to others.''

''And you pointed the way to Urmaal and Snurrl?''

''Indeed. You are very perceptive. We had always been close friends. Urmaal and Praal, my mate, had been littermates. I told them first of all.''

''And they rejected what you said.''

''No. Not at first. At first they too began to walk the way. They too had seen the Paradox face to face. It was . . . it was Urmaal who had delivered the deathblow to Praal. I . . . was unable to. They had seen and they knew.''

''Later, then?''

''Yes, later. They rejected my vision. They could not see clearly. They were blinded by too much love and too much life.''

''And you killed Snurrl.''

''No!'' Grrul shouted. ''No! I would never do such a thing! I am not guilty of that death!''

''Then who did kill Snurrl, Grrul? Your followers? Some poor Ranthrr you put up to it? Did you point him out and say, 'That one does not believe, that one must die'?'' Seeker's voice was hard and flat and filled with cold accusation.

Grrul moaned suddenly and buried his face in his hands. ''I didn't want it to happen like that! I didn't realize what they would do! I swear it! But I felt betrayed and angered and it must have shown to them. They . . .''

''They killed Snurrl because they thought you wanted him killed,'' Seeker declared harshly.

The old Ranth moaned piteously. ''Yes, yes! They sought

to rid me of something which pained me and in turn left me with an even greater pain! Oh, by the ancient Gods, Questioner, I'm guilty! Guilty not only of the death of Snurrl, but of the death of those five poor fools who died so brutally beneath the slashing claws of Urmaal's mad Blood Right! She slew them all! And she would have slain me, too, if she could have found me. But I fled to this cave that only I knew of. And here I slowly gathered my followers about me anew.''

"Urmaal will come now, Grrul. You know that. She will complete her Blood Right."

He nodded sadly. "It does not matter any longer. I am a very old Ranthrr. Over three hundred and fifty years. When you leave these caves, I too will leave them. I will go out into the desert at last and make my peace. I will walk the Lefthand Pathway to its end this time. I will transcend the Paradox."

Seeker stared silently at Grrul for several moments. "Just one more thing I don't quite understand. Why the organization on Ranthar? Why people like Fmaal/Ymaal?"

"I never meant for that to happen. But as I told the truth to more and more Ranth, problems arose. Like those with Snurrl and others. And those I taught, taught others of the Lefthand Pathway as well. It just grew and grew."

"And naturally the larger it got the more it had to defend itself against those who did not believe. The truth defending itself against the lie," Seeker commented ironically. "So an organization was created to spread and protect the faith. And naturally some were more zealous than others. As a result those who stood in the way sometimes were dealt with in a manner that had little to do with truth or transcendence. Am I right?"

Grrul nodded solemnly. "You have guessed correctly. But how could you possibly have known that?"

Seeker laughed out loud. "How did I know? You Ranth really are an egotistical race! By my six pouches, Grrul, all I did just then was recount the experience of every sapient species in the Federation!

"You faced death, Grrul, and didn't like what you saw. No creature can blame you for that. So you searched for a way to deny death, to transcend the Paradox, as you call it, to avoid the inevitable. And you stumbled on the Lefthand Pathway. It seemed a way out!

"And you believed, Grrul! You believed! Just as much as

the Ranth who wait and wait for immortality believe that it will come any day now. But your belief seemed so superior to you, because you yourself had felt its truth in your own mind. You had opened your eyes and seen the shining of its meaning!

"That is nothing rare, Grrul. It is the commonest thing in the universe. Next to death and arachnids, of course."

Grrul covered his face with his hands again. His shoulders were shaking with silent sobs. "It . . . my vision is not wrong. I know it is the truth!"

Seeker smiled. "It is *a* truth, Grrul. It is *your* truth. But that doesn't make it universal Truth, whatever in the universe that might be! To transcend death by finding another form of death, well, it may satisfy *you* and your followers. It may satisfy millions, for that matter. But is it really *the* answer? Or only a new way of asking the question?"

"What . . . are you suggesting, Questioner?"

"I am suggesting that you have *not* followed the logic unto death, Grrul, but only up to it. And then you shied away at the last moment."

"How could you know this?"

Seeker chuckled mirthlessly. "Because I have walked the face of Labyrinth, old Ranthrr. And there the logic goes unto death whether you will it to or not."

Grrul sat and stared at his hands. Trrulul lay crumpled on the floor, his eyes wide and staring in fear and confusion. Seeker watched them for a few seconds and then said to its host, "Well, I don't think there's anything else we need to know. Are you satisfied, Krral?"

Krral's tone was flat, hard, and tightly controlled. "No. But there's nothing more I want to know. Let's go." Seeker moved back into its portion of Krral's mind and gave the Ranthrr total control once more.

Krral stood looking down at Master Grrul. "I will tell Urmaal," he declared coldly. Then he turned and, without looking back, left the chamber. Behind him, he could hear the gentle weeping of Master Grrul. Or perhaps it was Trrulul.

# IV.

Whoever fights monsters
should see to it that in doing so
he does not himself become a monster.
Friedrich Nietzsche
Beyond Good and Evil

Urmaal sat quietly and stared into space. Krral sat just as quietly and watched her face closely.

Finally the Ranthaa focused her eyes and brought them to meet his. "So. He admits his guilt. And he is in that cavern complex near Terminus." She paused, looking off into vacant space again, and then murmured to herself, "After all these years of searching, it is that simple. Every track, every scent, indicated he had fled the planet. It was all false spoor, put down to confuse me. And so it did. I thought he had left and went out after him while he went to ground right there on Gobnar. So simple."

"What will you do?" Krral asked softly.

Urmaal suddenly looked very tired and very old. "Do? I will go and kill him. I will complete my Blood Right."

"Why?"

She focused sad eyes on his once more. "Why? Because it is something that must be done, something that must be completed. The four of us, Grrul, Praal, Snurrl, and I were friends, almost littermates. For all those years, we were almost inseparable. We even picked the same planet for our First Hundred duty. Then when Praal died so horribly we . . ." Her voice ran down. For several moments she was silent. Then she said softly,

"It must be completed. The circle must be closed. The game must be run to ground and its throat slashed."

"You'll never find him, Urmaal," Krral declared. "He's out there on the surface by now, in some cave. You'll never find him."

She smiled slightly. "Oh, I'll find him, all right. Don't worry about that. It is meant to be." She looked down at her hands and slowly bared her claws. "I'll find him," she muttered as if she were alone.

Krral nodded slowly. "And then you'll kill him," he stated, his voice flat and neutral.

"And then I'll kill him," she agreed.

"And then you'll be alone. The last of the four. All dead. All dead but you. What then, Urmaal?"

She was silent for a long, long time. Krral began to wonder if she had forgotten he was there. Finally, though, she murmured, so softly he had to strain to hear, "All alone. What then? What then? Why . . . I'll come back here and complete my Third Hundred then."

Krral shook his head. "They'll never let you. High Minister Shrryl will never let you back in the Service if you go and kill Grrul. It will cause too much of a furor. He's Master Grrul now and many Ranth on Gobnar and even other planets follow him. To kill him would make you outcast from the pride. You'd hunt alone until the day you died."

They sat for a long time without exchanging another word. Then Krral said gently, "Give it up, Urmaal. It's over. I should be furious with you for using me this way, you know. You set me up for this. Your whole purpose was to trace Grrul. You used Mraal the same way and she died. I almost did. Or worse, I was almost insane.

"I should be in a rage with you. I should be roaring and thrashing about, claws out and blood lust in my eyes. But somehow I can't bring myself to it.

"Give it up, Urmaal. Can't you see it makes no sense any longer? It doesn't matter."

"It matters," she said with sudden fierceness. "It's all that matters! My whole life I've waited for this moment, for the chance to fulfill my Blood Right and revenge Snurrl. Now I can do it! Yes, I used you. And I used Mraal. And I've used others in the past. And if you had failed, I would have used others after you! I will have Blood Right on the Ranthrr that killed Snurrl!''

''And so you will murder an old Ranthrr who weeps over his own crimes and who is not even capable of defending himself. Is that Blood Right? Or is that something else? Something sad and sick and twisted?

''They killed your mate, Urmaal. And I fear they killed something in you at the same time. You have searched for the last of those responsible for the murder of Snurrl for so long that you have become a murderer yourself. Give it up, Urmaal. You're only destroying yourself this way.''

Her expression was filled with despair. ''I can't, Krral. I can't. I must run the game to ground. I must. Or life loses all its meaning.'' She stood. ''Go now. I will be leaving almost immediately. Your investigation is finished. I know what I wanted to know. I'll have you reassigned.''

Krral stood. ''No. My investigation isn't over. I'm going to finish this thing, Urmaal. You've got what you wanted, but I don't. I haven't found Mraal's murderers yet.''

She shrugged. ''As you will. It doesn't matter to me any longer. Go. And thank you.''

Krral turned and walked to the door of Urmaal's office. He put his hand to the opening pad and then halted, turning slowly back to face her. ''Urmaal,'' he said in a voice barely above a whisper, ''if the only thing that has given your life meaning all these years is the death of Grrul, then your life has been nothing but one long death. That *can't* be right.''

There was nothing more to say, so he left.

# PART THREE

## *The Silence of the Heart*

# I.

⚜

*A man is always prey to his truths.*
*Once he has admitted them,*
*he can never free himself from them.*
    Albert Camus
    The Myth of Sisyphus

High Minister Shrryl nodded absently. "So, then, Urmaal has gone to Ranth-urrl-Gobnar to deal with this Master Grrul? Hmmmm, hmmmm, yes, yes. And you feel she intends to fulfill her Blood Right for the death of her mate Snurrl after all these years? My, how odd. Such an obsession. Who would have thought that Urmaal—calm, efficient Urmaal—would harbor such hatred in her heart? I would have wagered it would be a hot day on Vynnur before she would behave in such a way. Well, well, I guess one never really knows the heart of another. It can't be helped."

"I imagine nothing will come of it, High Minister. Grrul said he was going out onto the surface. If he does, there will be no way for Urmaal to trace him. I doubt she'll actually find him, much less kill him, if that's what worries you."

"No, no. It can't be helped. But you don't feel this Grrul and his followers represent any threat, eh?" The High Minister fixed Krral with an inquisitive stare for a brief moment, then looked down at all the paperwork on his desk. The Ranthrr was clearly more interested in his work than in Krral's report.

"Not really. I don't see his ideas spreading much beyond Gobnar. They work there, where death is so close. But here on Ranthar . . . well, they seem rather absurd."

"Naturally, yes, yes. And you don't think they had anything

to do with Mraal's murder, the death of Doctor Frryml, or all these suicides, then?''

Krral shook his head. "No. They have a few people here on Ranth to look out for their interests. I even suspect that they were mainly here to keep an eye on Urmaal. Grrul felt very guilty for Snurrl's death and . . .''

"Yes, yes, of course, Operative. And they acted against you because they knew Urmaal intended to use you to find them. I understand completely. But they're no threat. No threat. Good. But that still leaves open the question of the murders and the suicides, eh? Any ideas there? You are going to follow up, aren't you?''

"Yes, of course, High Minister. I have every intention of continuing my investigations if you'll allow it.''

"Yes, yes, of course. Permission granted. Go to it, Operative.'' He dug about on his desk for a second and then held up a small piece of note paper. "Here it is. Hmmmmm. Yes. Three more last week.'' He put the paper down and glared at Krral. "Yes. I want to find out all about this. It seems dangerous to me. Un-Ranthlike.'' He snorted. "Committing suicide! Not at all Ranth. Get to the bottom of it, Operative, and I daresay you'll find your murderers as well. Those who would take their own lives aren't likely to stick at taking someone else's.''

Krral nodded and sat silently for a moment. Then he spoke. "Sir, might I make a request?''

"Request? Certainly. What is it?''

"Could you possibly see your way to up my access rating? Perhaps to Status One?''

Shrryl frowned. "Status One? Hmmmmm. That's usually Commissioner level. Like Urmaal. Well, I suppose so. But only for the duration of this assignment. Then it's back down to Status Four again.'' He paused and gave Krral a quizzical look. "Ummmmm. By the way, how are you getting on with your, um, guest? I mean, the Questioner?''

"We're fine,'' Seeker responded. "Krral and I work well as a team, High Minister.''

"Hmmmm, yes, good, good. Well, be sure you, um, both keep me posted. No need for personal appearances. Memos at Status One are secure enough from now on. Yes. Well, I have many things to do, Operative,'' he said, glancing down at the papers that covered his desk. "If you'll pardon me . . .''

Krral rose, nodded, and went to the door of the room. As his hand touched the knob, Shrryl called after him. "Find them, Operative. Find out what's behind these murders and suicides. Most un-Ranthlike. And, I suspect, dangerous. We need to put a stop to it as soon as possible. These numbers keep increasing every month. Not good. We've kept a tight security lid on it so far, but sooner or later it's bound to leak. Not good. See to it, Operative."

With a nod, Krral opened the door and left.

Krral growled softly as he gazed at the data on the screen. "This trail's gone cold, Questioner. Doctor Frryml's been dead many weeks now and there's been enough time to wipe his tracks from the earth. Plus those of whoever killed him. Even the keenest eyes won't find any trace, I fear. Nor the sharpest nose catch scent of any spoor." He sighed and sat back.

"I'm afraid you're right," Seeker agreed. "So then let's ignore the good doctor's stale trail and concentrate on something else. The weapon that killed him. I think we should investigate two things. First, precisely what kind of dagger it is and where ones like it might be obtained right now. Second, whether or not the wounds on the Ranth who are committing suicide are similar to that on Doctor Frryml. By the way, I assume weapons were found with the suicide victims. Can we check that?"

"We should be able to. The Status One High Minister Shrryl gave me would access material like that. Let's try." He touched in commands on his keypad. Information began to glow to life on his datanet screen. "Hmmmmmm," he mused, looking at it. "That's odd, don't you think?"

"Very. No weapons found in the group suicides. But all died in the same way. A knife thrust between the left ribs, sideways into the heart. The flat of the blade was parallel with the horizon line. Very like Frryml's wound, except . . ."

"Except his was upward from the front and the blade perpendicular," Krral finished. "I can easily imagine how you would thrust one of those curved knifes between the ribs"— he touched the spot on his left side—"and even how the curve of the blade would bring the point right into your heart. The upward thrust is still impossible to imagine doing to yourself. But why no weapons in the group deaths? And look here at these individual suicides. Same wounds, no weapons. That seems so odd I can't imagine it wasn't one of the first things anyone who looked at this file previously would've noticed. Yet no one has even mentioned it to me.''

"But why no weapons?" Seeker wondered. "The wounds are the same and could have been inflicted with the same kind of knife that Frryml was murdered with. Why leave the dagger in Frryml's case and not in the group suicides?"

"Maybe," Krral said thoughtfully, "to make sure everyone thought it was an accident." He touched the keypad again. "Wonder if there are any other deaths where the weapon was left behind," he murmured. The data flashed on. "Ah. Five cases in the last four years. Let's check the wounds." He paused as he scanned the screen. "I'll be a simian," he muttered. "Same wound from an upward thrust. And they're all listed as accidents! Seems an awful lot of people have been tripping and falling on daggers."

Seeker considered. "Run a correlation on them, Krral. See if there is any connection between the five and Doctor Frryml. Check everything. What pride they come from, where they attended school, where their First Hundred was, what they did for their Second Hundred. Everything. Set it running. And then there's one other thing I want to check."

Krral's fingers flew over the keypad, touching in the commands for the correlation. "All right, it's being processed. Now what's the other thing?"

"You may not like this one, Krral. If not, I'll understand. I want to check Mraal's wounds."

"Ah," Krral said softly. "Of course. I should have thought of that. I can see why it's necessary." He touched the keypad and data came up on the screen. He gazed at it, his face drawn into a rigid mask of control. "Three wounds, Questioner, one in each of the vital areas. Looks like the first two thrusts didn't . . . didn't stop her. Then the last one must have . . . gone home." He paused and breathed deeply. "Damn. The bastards. She must have fought them like an ancient Ranthaa protecting her cubs. She was . . . always a very special Ranthaa, Questioner. You would have been proud to know her. She . . ." He stopped, his heart too full to continue.

"Krral," Seeker said gently. "Look. There was blood on her claws. Ask for an analysis. See if it was hers or not."

The Ranthrr called the data up. "Hers and not hers. Huh. She got in a few licks of her own at least."

"Would those licks have been serious wounds, Krral? Serious enough to be treated at a medical center?"

Krral hesitated. "Very possibly. Mraal's claws had been shaped like mine. She also was an adept in Dreadclaw. In fact, that's how we met. We were studying with the same Master on Ranth-urrl-Gobnar. Yes, a wound from her claws could be quite serious. I wasn't kidding Trrulul when I said I could rip off his face with one swipe, you know."

"Good. Then check the records of the medical centers for the day Mraal was killed. See if there were any treatments for cuts to the face area. That's what she would have gone for, right?"

"Right." Krral went to it with a will. Data came up and they gazed at it. "Damn," Krral muttered. "Not a thing."

"Hmmmmm," Seeker mused. "The records have been tampered with before. Check something else. Two things. Check to see who the doctors on duty were for the hours after Mraal's death. And check what antibiotic-type medicines were issued from the centers for halting infection."

When the data came on the screen and began to roll up, Krral cursed suddenly and hit the freeze button. "Look! Doctor Frryml! He wasn't on duty that day but he came in specially to handle a personal call! And you were right! The center pharmacy issued antibiotics at the same time and on his prescription!"

"Good, good," Seeker murmured. "Now see if we can find out who those medicines were issued to. And then we might want to pay someone a visit."

A light flashed slowly in the upper lefthand portion of the screen. "Huh," Krral grunted, "the correlation is ready on the murders. Let's give it a look." He touched in the command.

After a few moments he sat back and whistled softly. "Now *that*," he said softly, "is damn interesting. Frryml and three of the five all spent their First Hundred on Ranth-urrl-Vynnur. The other two spent part of their Second Hundred there.

"For your information, Questioner, Ranth-urrl-Vynnur is considered the worst of all the Ranth worlds. It's basically a lump of ice. Coldest place you can imagine. Even less atmosphere than Gobnar and mostly methane. Nobody wanders around its surface or hides out in caves! Whole planet is covered with about a mile-thick sheet of ice and blowing methane snow. There's doubt we'll ever be able to terraform it, but the fact is, it's very rich in some very rare elements, so we stay there. Hmmmmm. If I remember right, it's got the highest mortality rate of all the planets. Damn dangerous place for a First Hundred." He paused. "I . . . um . . . hope you don't think we should go there like we did to Gobnar?"

Seeker chuckled. "No. We went to Gobnar to find a very specific person. All these people on this list were here when they died. I see no need to go to Vynnur. At least not yet."

Krral groaned. "I don't like the sound of that. Well, what next, Questioner?"

"The name of the Ranth the medicine was issued to. And then I want to stop by the morgue again."

"The morgue? Whatever for? Frryml's body is long gone."

"The body, yes. How about the dagger?"

"Hmmmm. That should still be there."

"Can we get it for a while?"

"My Status One allows for that, yes. The attendant won't be happy about it. They hate letting anything go. Except the bodies, of course. But since it was judged an accident, there's no real reason to keep it as evidence. Yes, I can check it out. Have to bring it back, though."

"Fine. And then I want to go to the nearest museum to get a good look at some really old Ranth daggers. And see if we can't find out who might be making replicas."

Krral chuckled deep in his throat. "Why? Do you want to buy one? Are you thinking of committing suicide?"

Seeker's reply was solemn. "Not quite yet. But it might be interesting to see who has purchased replicas recently and find out if they are considering killing themselves. Or someone else."

The Ranthaa behind the desk was very old. Her fur had turned to silver around her muzzle, along her arms, and down her belly. Her eyes were deep and looked out on a world long studied and long understood. "The daggers? The one you seem to be referring to is a ceremonial dagger used for sacrifice to the Goddess/God Krrumaal. Comes from the Classical period on the northern landmass. A beautiful piece." She reached

behind her and took a large volume from a bookshelf. Placing
it on her desk, she opened it and swiftly and surely turned to
a well-worn section of the book. She reversed it so Krral could
see the plates that were there. "Prefer books to datanets," she
muttered. "Here. This is a sampling of similar daggers. More
or less the same period and area. All the same general 'S'
shape. Just different designs on the blades and hilts. They were
made of steel, you know. Heated, hammered, quenched in
blood, then heated, hammered, quenched again. The maker
folded them over again and again in the process. The result of
the layering is to give them amazing strength and phenomenal
sharpness. Magnificent pieces."

Krral stared at the pictures. They all looked the same to him.
But Seeker pointed out the different etching of the blades and
the varied ways the hilts were wrapped. "Huh," the Ranthrr
finally commented. "Dangerous-looking things. Could kill a
Ranth with one of those, I suspect."

The old Ranthaa chuckled. "Easily. One thrust. The curve
was made specially to carry the point between the ribs and then
into the heart of the victim. And they were so sharp it didn't
even take much effort."

"How many of these are still around?"

"You mean real ones? Hmmmmm. We have twenty here.
Might be another thirty with private collectors and in smaller
museums. No more than that. They're very old, and not many
things like that survived the Breakup, you know."

"Any way to get one?"

"An original? Ha! Not likely! They're rare and no one in
his right mind would part with one if he had it."

"Any ever get stolen?"

She gave him a hard look. "It's been done, but it's not easy.
Every one of them is known, photographed, catalogued, and
kept under lock and key. Anybody wants to study them, and
has the right credentials, they're available. But otherwise,
they're in vaults. These things are racial treasures, you know.
You couldn't sell a stolen one if you wanted to."

"Well, then, how about buying a replica?"

"Nothing easier! We sell them in the museum shop. Of
course, those are only half-size and used for decoration. But
they're very accurate replicas."

"No, I mean full-size ones. Like this." He pulled out the

dagger that he had gotten from the file at the morgue and handed it across to her.

She took it gingerly but with evident interest. After studying it a moment, she rose from her desk and went to a file cabinet on the other side of the room. She rummaged in one of the drawers for a moment, and then came back to her desk with a thick folder in her hands. "Paper. I like physical things, like books and files. This is all on datanet, of course. But I can't stand those things. Old-fashioned, but solid, that's what I like." She opened the file and searched through it. "Aha!" she finally announced. "Here it is!" She held out a picture to Krral. "Your dagger."

Krral studied the photograph. It was indeed the dagger that lay on the desk between them. "You mean that thing is an original?"

She chuckled. "No, no, just a copy. But a very, very good copy. Best I've seen in a long time. Whoever made it is a real stickler for details." She picked it up and held it out to him, pointing at the blade. "See those indentations? Those are hammering marks. The ancient Ranth thought they were beautiful. Most replicas exclude them. But whoever made this one included them. Very nice work. But, you see, this one was moulded, not hammered. Hmmmmm. Now that I think on it, the mould for this could only have come from the original. I wonder who has it?" She turned back to the file for a second. "Ah, here. Private collector, one Damurrl. Yes, yes, I think I remember meeting him once at a conference. Hmmmmm, says here he actually has three of them. Plus quite a nice collection of other Classical artifacts as well, I seem to recall."

"Interesting," Krral responded. "Any idea who made this replica? I'd like to get another. This belongs to a friend who got it from his pride mother when she died. Has no idea where she got it. Do you?"

She frowned slightly. "Work that good isn't common. I know, because I had to find someone to make our copies for the displays and the half-sized version we sell in the shop." She turned to a file box on her desk and opened it. "Hmmmmm. Here are the ones I contacted. List of some seven. You might try them to see if they did the work. Or they might know who did."

Krral copied down the names. "Thank you."

"Easier way, you know," she said cryptically.

"Easier way?"

"Easier than running around to seven different foundries and trying to get someone who'll talk to you. Just get ahold of this Damurrl, the Ranthrr who owns the original. Whoever made the copy had to borrow his to make the mould. No other way to copy those hammer marks so accurately. He must know who he loaned it to, eh?" She smiled secretly.

Krral smiled back. "Right. Thanks. You've been very helpful."

Her smile broadened and took on an impish quality. "Quite all right, Operative. Always glad to help the Service. And don't wonder how I knew what you are. Been around as long as I have, you'll know an operative when you see one, too. Heh, heh, you all have a certain look about you. Well, good luck. And remember one thing." Her face became suddenly solemn. "I know you'll think it's just the superstition of an old Ranthaa, but these daggers are dangerous things. They were used for evil purposes many eons ago when we were a primitive and violent race. They still carry something of that aura around with them. They stir strange parts of our racial memory. I don't know why you're interested in them and I really don't care. But just be careful, Operative. Just be careful."

Damurrl was early in his Third Hundred. He was a tall Ranthrr, with dark golden colored fur and a black blaze that was beginning to grey on his chest. From the way he moved, Krral knew he was an adept in one of the fighting arts. Not a Ranthrr to fool with.

But he was all cordiality. He looked closely at the dagger Krral offered, then went and brought the original, setting the two side by side. "On its own, the copy looks pretty good," he said in his quiet, confident voice. "But next to the original, you can see how shabby it is."

Krral stared at the original dagger. It was magnificent indeed. And the old Ranthaa at the museum had been correct. It did stir strange feelings deep within him. He brought his mind sharply back to business before Seeker could remind him. "Indeed. It's . . . I guess lovely is the wrong word. Perhaps impressive would be better."

Damurrl laughed. "Impressive is as good as any. They're

strange things, these daggers. You can feel the danger in them, sense the blood flowing, the life slipping away. I have three of them, all from the Classical period. This is my favorite.''

"Can you remember who made the mould which mine came from?"

"Oh, yes. It was a Doctor Frryml. He was an amateur enthusiast for the Classical period. Met him at a convention about six years ago. He made a mould of this dagger right here in this room.'' He frowned. "Said he would only make one copy, for himself, and then break the mould.'' He eyed Krral's dagger as it lay on the table top. "Unless this is it, he lied.''

Krral nodded. "I'm afraid he did. Do you know who he took the mould to for the casting? I have seven names. Would any of them mean anything to you?''

Damurrl took the list from Krral and studied it. "I know most of these names. Seen their work at the conventions. Only one here good enough for work like this is Branrrul. He specializes in really fine work of the Classical period, mostly jewelry and small statuary. I can't say for sure that he did it, but he's capable of it so I'd bet a good bit on it.'' He handed the list back to Krral. "I'd check with him. And if he did make it, tell him I want that mould broken. No more without my explicit permission. When I see Doctor Frryml again I will give him a very severe talking-to!''

When Krral left, Damurrl sat looking at his dagger for several moments. Then he rose and went to his commnet. He touched in a code number. The screen lit up, but stayed blank. "Yes?" a voice said from the empty screen.

"Damurrl. Krral was just here.''

"Ah. With the dagger?''

"Yes. I sent him to Branrrul.''

"Excellent. We will see to it at once.''

"Be careful. Krral is dangerous. I can sense he is an adept in one of the arts. I didn't see his claws, so I don't know which.''

"We are aware of Krral's abilities. He will be dealt with carefully. And finally. Peace and endless sleep.''

"Endless sleep without dreams,'' Damurrl intoned. Then he turned off the commnet and went back to sit in front of the dagger, gazing at it fondly, his eyes slowly caressing its flowing, deadly lines.

* * *

The Branrrul foundry was on the edge of a medium-sized industrial complex. The building was fairly large and mostly empty. No one was around except for the Second Hundred Ranthrr in the office at the front of the building. He claimed to be Branrrul, but something about him alerted Krral's ancient hunting senses. He was a heavily built Ranthrr and looked powerful, if a bit slow. Krral felt sure he could handle him if any trouble arose. But the whole place was so quiet, so empty of Ranth or activity, it made the operative even more alert than usual. In his mind, Seeker sensed its host's tension and carefully monitored every sense, doubling the search for possible danger.

Branrrul turned the dagger over and over in his hands. "Yes, this is one of ours. I remember it well. Nice piece. Fellow brought a mould in, direct from the original."

"Remember who it was?"

"Sure. Can't forget jobs like this one. Ranthrr named Doctor Frryml, works in one of the medical centers. Said he was an enthusiast for the Classical period. Odd thing, though."

"Odd? In what way?"

"Well, why in the world would a doctor, even an enthusiast, want a run of a hundred replica Classical period sacrificial daggers? Give 'em to his friends for presents, or something?" He shrugged dismissively. "I don't know. Just seems odd, that's all. But we just fill the orders and don't ask questions. Nothing illegal about it, so we just filled the order."

"You make them here?"

"Sure. Want to see where? Mould is still out in the shop. Be glad to show you. Even break it up while you're watching so you can tell Damurrl I did what he asked. Nothing going on right now so it's pretty deserted, but all the equipment is there." He casually threw the dagger on the desk and stood. Then he walked to a door at the back of the office and motioned Krral to follow.

On the other side of the door was a large room, perhaps forty feet deep by thirty wide. Racks covered the walls and were piled with all sorts of equipment, including grey lumps that Krral assumed must be moulds. In the center of the room was an electronic furnace. Here and there, in the open space around the furnace, were piles of metal bars and other things Krral couldn't guess the use of.

As they walked toward the furnace, Krral felt a prickling between his shoulder blades. *Something's strange here, Questioner,* he said silently.

*Agreed,* Seeker replied. *We must be extra alert. If something happens, however, I'll get out of your way so you can do whatever you have to do.*

*Good,* the operative replied grimly. *If anything happens, it'll probably happen very swiftly.*

Branrrul gestured at the furnace. "Electronic. Gets to over five thousand degrees in about two minutes. One of the best on Ranthar." Krral stopped next to the furnace and studied it briefly. Branrrul walked over to one of the racks and took off a greyish shape. "Here," he said, turning back and bringing it to Krral. "This is the mould for Doctor Frryml's dagger."

Krral took it and studied it. It was made of some dense metal and came apart easily into two halves. Inside was the shape of the dagger.

He was about to hand the mould back to Branrrul when a slight sound caught his attention. *Company,* Seeker announced in his mind. Krral turned his head slightly to better see around him, but still keeping part of his attention on Branrrul. Three more Ranthrr had appeared from among the racks and piles of material.

Branrrul held out his hand. "Here, give the mould to me. You won't be needing it any more where you're going."

"Oh?" Krral said, his voice firm. "And where am I going?"

Branrrul chuckled nastily. "Into the furnace, Krral. At five thousand degrees, there won't be a thing left of you. Not even cinders. Nothing to find, nothing to trace. You just disappear completely, mysteriously. End of investigation."

"They'll just send out another."

"I doubt it. Urmaal's gone now. Shyrrl's not really all that keen on the whole thing, no matter what he says. No, I imagine you're the last Service operative we'll see around here. Now give me the mould like a good cub. And we'll be about our business swiftly and efficiently."

Branrrul held out his right hand again. With his left, he reached into the pouch on his harness and pulled out a dagger. Out of the corner of his eye, Krral could see the other three pull out identical daggers.

"Did you kill Mraal, too?"

"Mraal? No. I don't kill Ranthaa. Only Ranthrr who become too nosy."

"Like Doctor Frryml? He was killed by a lefthanded Ranthrr, Branrrul. And you're holding your dagger in your left hand."

Branrrul growled deeply. "You're too damn smart for your own good. Not that it matters any more. No, Frryml wasn't nosy. Just stupid and inconvenient. He failed in his task and started to panic. We had no choice."

"We?"

Branrrul growled. "That's enough questions. Give me the mould now." The other three had moved closer, until they were within a few feet of striking distance.

Krral moved suddenly, flinging one piece of the mould directly at Branrrul's head. It struck square on the Ranthrr's forehead and he tumbled backward with a howl of pain. At the same instant, Krral spun around and threw the second half of the mould at the closest Ranthrr, hitting him in the shoulder and making him stagger back.

The operative stepped quickly against the furnace to cover himself from behind. The Ranthrr on his left leapt toward Krral, his dagger, held in his right hand, swinging a shimmering overhead arc. Krral stepped toward his attacker and slightly to his right, his own right hand shooting up at an angle to deflect the strike. As their arms touched, Krral spun on his right foot, bringing his left hand around in a sweep, claws extended. His blow slashed into the Ranthrr's head, ripping off one ear and spraying gore and blood in a great fountain. Krral swiftly kicked the staggered opponent in the right hip with his left foot, sending him sprawling into the second Ranthrr.

The third was almost on him. This one knew better than to swing his knife overhead so foolishly. He held the dagger with the blade coming out of the top of his fist and jabbed at Krral with it, trying to drive the steel into his guts. Krral swayed to the right, the blade barely skimming past him. His right hand swung around with the motion of his hips and swiped at his opponent's face. The extended claws ripped the left side of the Ranthrr's muzzle off. Then, as he stumbled past, Krral continued his movement by spinning to the left on his right foot. His left foot came up and slammed into the back of the Ranthrr's head.

The second Ranthrr had disentangled himself from his companion, who had collapsed unconscious on the floor. He took one look at the situation, decided he didn't like the odds, and with a curse, flung his dagger at Krral. The operative dodged easily and the Ranthrr turned and ran.

Krral was about to follow when he heard a groan from Branrrul. He was coming to. Krral stepped quickly to him and grabbed him by his harness. He pulled him over to the furnace. Studying the piece of equipment carefully, Krral reached out and flipped what looked like a starting switch, then turned a dial which indicated temperature up to the highest setting. That finished, he checked on the other two Ranthrr. The first one was dead. Krral's blow had been a bit further back on the head than planned and had smashed in the back part of the skull. The other one was also dead. The kick had broken his spine right at the base of the skull. "Sloppy," Krral muttered to himself.

Branrrul moaned again. Krral stepped to him. "At least I've still got you around to talk with," he grumbled. The Ranthrr's eyes fluttered open and stared into Krral's for a moment in total disorientation. "Yeh," Krral growled. "It's me. Your buddies didn't do too well."

Branrrul tried to sit up. Krral grabbed him by the harness and lifted him to his feet. He held his face nose to nose with Branrrul's and uttered a feral growl. "Look, stupid, the furnace is on. I've turned it up all the way. Just like you planned to do for me. Only things have changed since you made your original plans. Now you're going to tell me things I want to know. And if you don't have the answers I like, I'm going to stick your hands in the furnace first, then your feet, and right on up your body until you tell me all I want. Understand?"

"You . . . wouldn't," Branrrul quavered.

Krral laughed evilly. "Try me. Just look into my eyes, Branrrul, and tell me what you see. That's it. Take a good look. It's your death that's there, friend, and it's not a pretty one, either. Slow and painful. Now, are we talking, or do I start cooking you?"

Branrrul whimpered. "I don't know anything. I'm nobody. I just do what they tell me."

"They? Who's they?"

"I don't know. I really don't. They just call. The screen's a blank. Even the voice sounds filtered."

"Brranth piss." He leaned over quickly and opened the door to the furnace chamber. The heat spewed out. "Good and hot, Branrrul. Nobody knows better than you how hot, eh? What's it going to be? Information or barbeque?"

"I'm being straight with you!" Branrrul wailed in fear. "By pride's honor, I swear it! I made the daggers for Frryml. They paid me well and it was good work. When they said to kill him, I went to his place with the excuse that someone was asking about the daggers. I killed him. That's all. Beyond that I don't know anything."

Krral sighed. "So people you don't know anything about just call you up on the commnet and you kill ex-customers like Doctor Frryml and visitors like me, eh? This is going to be a long session, I can tell. And I really hate the stench of burning flesh." He slammed his fist into the side of Branrrul's head, driving the Ranthrr suddenly to his knees. Branrrul grunted with surprise and pain. Krral grabbed his hand and began to push it toward the furnace door.

Branrrul screamed suddenly in terror and gave a great surge. He was a strong Ranthrr and panic gave him extra power. Krral, surprised by the suddenness and strength of the move, was thrown off balance and staggered back.

Branrrul threw himself at Krral in a fury. The operative coolly sidestepped and slammed a closed fist into his opponent's face, then drove the other into his side at about heart level. Branrrul was stunned by the blows and staggered backward. He lost his balance and, with a scream, fell heavily backward toward the furnace. Krral made a desperate grab for his harness and missed.

With a second scream, Branrrul slammed into the furnace. His head hit where the open door was. His scream was cut short as the five thousand degrees of heat burned his head to a cinder in an instant. The rest of the body, twitching spasmodically, topped by the smoking remnant of the Ranthrr's head, slumped to the floor next to the furnace.

Krral stood and stared in dismay at the body. "Damn," he finally muttered. "There goes my lead. Sorry, Questioner. He might have given us some good information."

"I doubt it," Seeker said quietly. "He seemed sincere. He was frightened enough to be honest."

Krral shrugged. "What now?"

"Now I think we see who Damurrl called after we left. And I think we check on who has called our headless friend there. Maybe we can get closer to the source of all this trouble that way. Also, let's check the morgue again."

"The morgue? What for?"

"I got a good look at that third Ranthrr. And I have the feeling that we'll find him at the morgue. Another victim of a strange accident involving a dagger."

# II.

It was not until late the next day that the third Ranthrr that had attacked Krral showed up in the morgue, the victim of an unfortunate accident involving a dagger. Branrrul never showed up anywhere. All of which proved nothing and gave neither Krral nor Seeker any new clues to pursue.

A search of the files at the medical center turned up the name of the Ranth who had received antibiotics on the day of Mraal's murder. There were three in total and they decided to check all of them out.

The first turned out to be a Ranthrr who had been severely bitten by his pet Ranthum, a small, domesticated hunting felinoid of sometimes undependable temperament. The poor beast had had to be put to sleep since it had attacked the Ranthrr's mate as well and had been judged to be dangerous.

The second was a Ranthaa who had gashed her foot on a piece of jagged metal that was hidden by high weeds in the field where she had been cavorting with several cubs under her care. Krral had found her very attractive and made a mental note of her address for use once the case had been concluded.

The final recipient was a name that Krral recognized once he had thought about it for a while. "Drrulum. Hmmmm. I know this one, Questioner," he mused as they rode in the public shuttle car toward the address. "Come across him a few times. Petty thief, maladjusted, mildly neurotic. Been treated several times, but without his consent, not much more than that can be done. Never enough of a danger to society to require a personality restructuring. One of those rare marginal types we learn to tolerate in the name of greater freedom for the rest of us. He's been in fights, brawls, things like that. But somehow I can't picture him murdering anyone.''

They finally arrived at the address. The name next to the announcer pad wasn't Drrulum's, but that didn't really surprise Krral. He touched the pad. A tight voice, frightened and somewhat blurred, as if with drink, came from the commnet speaker next to the pad. But the small screen just above it stayed blank. ''Yeh? Whaddaya wan with me? Who's it, anyway? Huh?''

''Open up, Drrulum,'' Krral commanded sternly. ''This is official Service business. I've got Status One so I can force entry if I want to. So just open up and make this easy for all of us.''

''Drrulum? Ya want Drrulum? This ain't Drrulum. I'll open, but I ain't Drrulum and Drrulum ain't here.'' The door hissed and opened.

They walked into the most chaotic dwelling space Seeker had ever seen. It was filled with odds and ends of junk stacked and piled all over the available floor space. There appeared to be no order or logic to either the arrangement or to the things that had been collected. In addition, the smell of stale food permeated the air. Krral wrinkled his nose. ''What a stench!'' he growled. Peering through the gloom of the crowded space, he spied a figure sprawled listlessly on a rather dowdy chair. Both the chair and the Ranthaa (for that's what Krral finally decided it was) had seen much better days. The Ranthaa's medium brown fur was unkempt, matted, and dull and even balding over her shoulders. Her face was slack, somewhat puffy, and bore little sign of intelligence. Her eyes were dim and watery and empty of any expression.

As Krral approached, wending his way carefully through the stacks of refuse and keeping a lookout for possible piles of rotting food, the Ranthaa looked at him with disinterested eyes. ''He ain't here, if you want Drrulum. Bastard ain't been here for weeks. Gone off and left his mate behind, that's what the bastard's done,'' she whined piteously.

Krral looked down at her sprawling form, disgust wrinkling

his nose. "Any idea where he might be? Who was he working for last?" He flicked out his claws and waved them casually in the air. "Come on, think! You've got an idea, I'll bet."

She eyed the claws nervously. "I ain't seen him at all since the accident. Honest I ain't. He just upped and left, leaving his poor mate to fend for herself."

Krral growled softly. "Brranth piss! Poor mate, my bloody dew claw! You can get all the food you need just by going to the public kitchens." He looked around the room. "This place is a simian sty! You live like an animal! What is all this junk?"

"Junk?" she mumbled, gazing around with apprehensive eyes. "Junk? Ain't no junk. Just my things. Things I pick up. I need them, you know. They're nice things."

"Drrulum hides out here when things get hot, doesn't he?" Krral declared. "But this time things got so hot he had to find a better place."

*Ask about the accident she mentioned,* Seeker silently suggested. *Sounds like something someone might need antibiotics for.*

Krral nodded and asked, "What accident did Drrulum have that made him leave?"

She hunched down further into the chair. "Said I ain't supposed to talk about it to no one," she mumbled. "Drrulum might do somethin' to me if I says anythin'."

Krral reached down and gently rested his claws on her throat. "And I," he said with a fierce intensity that came out almost a growl, "will definitely do somethin' to you if you don't give me answers. Now what was the accident?"

She whimpered and muttered, "Fell down."

"Scratched his handsome face pretty badly, huh?"

"Yeh. Real mess. All kinds of claw . . . scratchmarks."

"Yeh. So bad he had to take antibiotics for them, huh?"

She nodded slightly, afraid to move against the claws which pressed so firmly against her skin. "Yeh. He was takin' some kinda pills. But I don't know nothin' else. Pride's honor I don't. So don't hurt me, O.K.?"

"Who was he working for when he had his fall? He's always doing little jobs for people. Who was it this time? Come on, now, think!" He flexed his claws slightly and they dug into her neck. She whimpered again.

"I . . . foggy memory. Some name . . . sort of like his own.

Doing work for him for a while. Pretty good pay. Wouldn't say what.''

''Name like his own? Wouldn't be anything like Damurrl, would it?''

She paused, trying to gather her thoughts, frowning in concentration. ''Damurrl? Dunno. Might be. Sounds right. But I ain't real sure. Foggy memory.''

''He was doing work for Damurrl,'' Krral declared flatly. ''Then he fell down and got all scratched up and went into a better hiding place. Right?''

She muttered incoherently for a few moments. ''Yeh. Somethin' like that. He went and left his mate.'' She snuffled as if about to cry.

*What do you think, Questioner? Seems like that's about all we'll get out of this one.*

Seeker hesitated. *What's wrong with her, Krral? She doesn't seem to be able to concentrate very well. And she seems to be sick or something. I've never seen a Ranthaa like this one before.*

Krral snarled softly. *A few Ranth take drugs, Questioner. They're weak creatures who can't deal with the world. The good or the bad part of it. Some defect in their minds, I guess. They use the drugs as a way out, a way to retreat and hide. By the looks of this one, I'd say she was taking Ixnoraline, which is made from the seeds of a plant that grows on Ranth-urrl-Urthar. Used in our medical technology for several purposes, mostly as a narcotic and relaxant. Maybe she spent her First Hundred on Urthar and got into the habit of chewing the seeds. Some Ranth do. She can get the stuff free at the medical center.* He gave her a disgusted look. *Pride only knows what she was once. Now she's just refuse.*

*I wonder,* Seeker mused. *Whatever, I don't think we'll get much more out of her as long as she's like this. Will she come out of it soon?*

The Ranthrr snorted. *Could be hours, even days. Depends on how much she took. The drug sort of meters itself out in the system, the effects wearing off slowly. In any case, we don't have time to wait. I think it might be worthwhile to check out our friend Damurrl again and see just how much he knows.*

*All right,* Seeker replied calmly. *I agree there doesn't seem to be much for us here. And the environment is hardly conducive*

*to remaining for long. I must say, Krral, I find far more varia-
tion among you Ranth than I had been led to believe existed.
One tends to think of you as all being perfectly happy. That
hardly seems to be the case.*

*The sane ones are,* Krral growled. *Only a very small minority, a crazy minority, aren't.*

Seeker made no reply.

Krral looked down at the Ranthaa again. "All right. I think
I know where my friend Drrulum might have gone to ground.
But if you see him before I do, tell him to give Krral a call. I
want to talk to him and I'll be a lot gentler if he comes to me
than if I have to waste a lot of time digging him out. Just tell
him that. He'll know what I mean."

Krral gave her one last gentle touch with his claws. Then
he sheathed them once again, turned and threaded his way back
across the room and out the door.

The Ranthaa stayed slumped in her chair for several moments
after the door closed behind him. Then she rose slowly and
shuffled over to a commnet that was on the far wall, almost
hidden behind piles of junk. She touched in a number and the
screen hummed to life, but no picture showed. "Yes, yes?"
came a stern voice. "What do you want?"

"Krral came, sir."

"Well, well. He is being most industrious, I must say. Following up every clue, eh? Good, good. Did you send him to
Damurrl again? That's our most obvious link, you know. He
must look more closely into that."

"Yes, sir. I hinted at a name like Drrulum's and he immediately mentioned Damurrl. I believe he is on his way there
right now."

"Good, good. Well, then, we shall see. Very well done.
Yes. You may leave now."

"Yes, sir." She turned from the screen and moved back to
the chair, her motions now more normal. Her face showed
clear intelligence, even determination. And her eyes glowed
with both humor and character.

From behind the chair where she had so lately sprawled, she
took a black bag. From within it, she pulled out a large mirror
and a comb. She began to comb her fur while she muttered to
herself. "Damn mess. Take hours to make it shine again. Damn
matted mess." She turned the mirror to her shoulders and

winced at the sight. ''Pride's honor!'' she cursed with heartfelt anger. ''It'll take a month for that to grow out again! Damn! They were a little bit too thorough.''

She spent about an hour with the comb and mirror. When she was finished, she left the room, the bag over her shoulder. She looked very different from the Ranthaa who had slumped in front of Krral just a short time before.

It was late evening when they arrived once more at Damurrl's place. Damurrl's was a rather large structure, placed on a hill, with heavy forest at its back and a view toward a series of lakes in the distance out its front. Like all the Ranth structures Seeker had seen to this point, it was one story high, and made from pressed earth stabilized with some complex acrylic compounds. The insides of all these residential buildings were vaguely cavelike and organic, a look the Ranth seemed to like. Perhaps, the ursoid thought, it reminds them of the dens they once inhabited. They certainly exude a certain earthy coziness, Seeker had to admit.

Krral walked around the building from a distance to scout the lay of the land. ''Just in case,'' he muttered to Seeker. ''Big place,'' he observed when he had completed his circuit. ''Damurrl lives well.''

''I don't understand that, Krral,'' Seeker said. ''If everything is provided for everyone, why is it that some Ranth seem to have so much more than others? The difference between the way that Ranthaa we talked to lives and the way Damurrl lives is rather extreme.''

Krral nodded. ''Of course. All Ranth, once they fulfill their First Hundred obligation on the colony worlds, have a right to food, medical care, housing, all the necessities of life. But what is provided is minimal. Most Ranth want more than the minimum. To get that, you have to work during your Second Hundred. The vast majority of Ranth would work in any case, simply because it's more interesting than just lying around all day. But by working, we can also earn extra credits and buy more things. It sort of adds an extra incentive.

''Naturally, some Ranth work harder or are smarter than others and so they earn more and can buy more. Some just can't find a place where they fit. Some give up and turn to drugs. There are all types, Questioner. All types. But no Ranth has to starve to death, or suffer from disease, or go without shelter. We tolerate the differences and the inevitable inequities they bring because without them, well,'' he shrugged, ''boredom and a general bland uniformity would be the result. We aren't some kind of intelligent social hymenopterids, you know.''

Seeker considered. ''So then there are social and economic differences, and drives like ambition and pride, and all the conflicts those things bring. All of which means, to be more specific, that there is a likely to be gap between possibility and actuality.''

Krral frowned. ''Those are pretty big terms. But if you mean that everyone doesn't get everything they want and that that makes some of them mad or unhappy or whatever, yeh. Pride's honor, Questioner, if it wasn't for that, we wouldn't need a Service and I wouldn't have a job.''

''Then there is crime.''

''Yeh. Nothing big and bloody, usually. Murder is . . . was very rare. Mostly petty things until . . . all this mess got going.'' He paused. ''I know I shouldn't pry, but have you got any idea what's going on here? I admit I'm stumped. I've even got this weird feeling I just can't shake that we're sniffing on the wrong trail.''

''Nothing firm yet, Krral. It isn't a simple situation. First, your whole culture is rather different than the image I originally had of it. But I'm becoming convinced this issue of suicide is, well, somehow tied to the things we heard on Gobnar. I don't know yet for sure. Just a growing sense of certainty. We need to talk to someone who knows it from the inside the way Master Grrul knew the Lefthand Pathway. I have a sense that the two are more closely connected than appears to be the case on the surface. And that somehow the whole issue of murder ties into that relationship as well.''

Krral cocked his head quizzically to one side. ''Murder, suicide and the Lefthand Pathway all connected? Sounds very odd to me. I can't see any connection at all. Except that connection between the method of the suicides and the method of the murders. But Grrul? I don't see that at all. And what about Mraal's murder? It seems to fit with the suicide/murder side of the equation.''

''Seems,'' Seeker admitted. ''But again, I'm not certain.

There are still several very large pieces of information missing. Until we get some of them in place, the best I can do is guess. And that's not what I'm supposed to be doing.''

The Ranthrr nodded and turned his attention back to Damurrl's abode. "Looks very quiet. Wonder if he's even there." He gave a short, harsh laugh. "That's something I hadn't planned on, him not being home."

"Can we get in his home even if he isn't there?" Seeker asked.

"Can, but shouldn't. Status One gives me access when someone is present. I'd have to have Status B or A to enter when no one was there."

The Questioner chuckled softly. "But there is a way in, isn't there? I can see the idea forming in your mind even as you make your official denials."

Krral grinned a little sheepishly. "Yeh, I guess so. It's not Service procedure, at least not official procedure. But there's a way to fiddle with the access lock and get in. Some of the operatives know it. But you can get in real hot water for using it . . . if you get caught." He hesitated. "So first we check to see if Damurrl's there. Then, if not, we go in anyway and see what we can find."

They left the cover of the forest and walked boldly up to the front entrance of Damurrl's home. As Krral had surmised, no one was in. "Must not have a mate," the operative murmured, "or at least if he does, she's not around right now. Well, then, it's in we go on our own."

He bent down to the entry keypad and began to touch the keys in a particular sequence. "Locks aren't much on Ranth. Just a sort of formality. There's a logic to these things," he muttered under his breath. "Once you get the first part of the sequence, the rest always falls into place. Hmmmmm. Hmmmmm. There! That's it! Now it must go this way. Right. And then finally . . . oooppps, no. There's a little twist to this one. Hmmmmm. Maybe this. Yes!'' The door slid open and they stepped into the darkened entry hall. Krral reached behind him and touched the door closure. The door hissed shut and they were plunged into a stygian blackness.

Like all his species, Krral's night vision was exceptional. In a few moments, his eyes had adjusted and he was easily able to pick his way down the entry hall to the large room where they had met Damurrl the first time. Moving carefully around it without disturbing anything, he passed through to the further regions of the house. His plan was to make a quick tour of the whole place to see where things were and then pick the spot that seemed most likely to have the most information for a more detailed search.

Beyond the main room were three more rooms. One was for food storage and preparation. The second was a library of sorts, filled with Damurrl's collection of Classical period artifacts, books on several topics, and a desk area where he obviously worked and conducted his business. The third and final chamber, aside from toilet and bath facilities, was clearly a bedroom.

When they had made their tour and returned to the main room, Seeker asked, "Is there any way to check the calls he's made in the last few days? Perhaps he has some sort of place where he keeps code numbers or something?"

Krral nodded. "Probably has most of them stored in the commnet's memory. Easy enough to check." He walked up to the keypad and began to fiddle with it. A list of names and numbers appeared on the screen. "Huh. There. That's his personal list. Any of those names mean anything to you?" They carefully scrutinized the list. It was about twenty-five names long. None of them were familiar.

Suddenly Seeker let out a pleased sigh. "Ah, so that's it."

"That's what?" Krral asked. "Sounds like you figured something out. How about sharing it?"

"That fifth name. Ludrrum. Look familiar?"

"Ludrrum? No. Should it be?"

"Look at the letters. Try making another name with them."

"Hmmmmm. Ludrrum? Murrdul? Drrulum? Ah! By all the Brranth on Urthar! Drrulum! And that one there, 'Lyfmrr,' that's Doctor Frryml!"

"Right. And I'll wager some of the others are the same. We should make a copy so we can work it out later. But it seems likely that if we want to get ahold of our friend Drrulum, we'll find him at the other end of that commnet connection." Following Seeker's suggestion, Krral took a pad and pen from the pouch on his harness and copied down the names and numbers.

They then searched the rest of the main room. Nothing of interest showed up, so they went on to the library. Krral went through the desk with great precision, removing each item in a careful sequence, scrutinizing it, and then replacing it in exactly the same location and position he had taken it from.

Two very interesting things turned up. The first was a receipt from Branrrul for payment for casting replica daggers. The second was a scrap of paper, stuffed way in the back of one cubbyhole, crumpled and smudged, with one name on it: Mraal. The sight of that name brought a feral snarl to Krral's lips. "The bastard," he rumbled. "He was involved, Questioner! No doubt about it!"

"Slim evidence, Krral. Too slim to rip someone's muzzle off, as you're thinking of doing right now. I agree it indicates some sort of link, but the question is, what sort of link? I don't believe Damurrl is the head of whatever is going on. Part of the machinery, perhaps. But not the motor that drives the whole thing. He's a way of getting where we want to go, but he's just a short stop on the journey. But I agree it might be very interesting to interview him more closely."

"The receipt from Branrrul and Doctor Frryml's name in his directory indicates he was lying about his relationship to the daggers," Krral said. "And since Frryml was killed with one of those same daggers, it all ties in very tightly. Questioner, there's no doubt this Damurrl is involved with both the suicides and the murders. Maybe even that of Mraal."

"Very possible. But somehow I think it's more complicated than that. Let's look around this room some more."

They combed the room carefully. On one of the display shelves, amidst a collection of clay figurines, they found something odd. It was a small stone, in the form of an irregular ovoid, perhaps four inches along the long axis. Krral picked it up and stared at it. It felt unusually heavy in his hand. "Any idea what it is?" Seeker asked. "Seems out of place in the midst of those other things."

Krral studied it. "Odd thing. Natural. Not shaped. Certainly not anything from the Classical period. Hmmmmm. I'm not even sure it's from Ranthar, Questioner. Like every Ranth, I've studied Rantharian geology. Don't remember anything like this. Strange." He paused. "Could be he picked it up during his First Hundred on whatever colony world he was serving on. Yeh. That could be. Sort of a memento. Lots of Ranth pick up keepsakes like that. I've got a Quurlmann Nut at home. Question is, which world did this rock come from? Of course, we can check his file and see what it says about his First Hundred service. But I'm beginning to have less and less faith in those files. Be interesting to see if the rock really is from the same place where the file says he spent his First Hundred." He opened his pouch and took out a small clear bag and a knifelike scraper. "Maybe I can scratch off a tiny bit for analysis so we can find out where it's from." Finished, he put the rock back in its place.

When they had completed the library, they gave the food area a quick going-over and then moved into the bedroom. Krral expertly went through the clothes storage drawers that were fitted in one wall. Then he searched through a closet area in another wall. Damurrl was frugal in the matter of clothes, as were most Ranth. He had no more than seven different harnesses, all of excellent craftsmanship, with matching pouches. His footwear was of good quality, but nothing outstanding. He had several cloaks for colder weather. Beyond that, nothing of note.

Finished, they returned to the main room. "Think we've done all there is to do. Also, I think we'd be wise to get out now before he comes back." Krral chuckled. "Love to meet him in the dark, but I'd prefer it when I'm on a little stronger legal grounds. The Service will often look the other way if an operative does things like this. But if we get caught doing it, the High Minister has to censure us. Especially for someone like Damurrl, who has something of a name and reputation. So I think it's time to call the hunt off for the moment." He stretched and yawned. "I could use some sleep in any case."

"You're sure there are no other places to look?" Seeker asked. "Nothing we've missed?"

"Nothing. Oh, well, there is one thing, but I doubt it's worth bothering with."

"What is it?"

"Well, generally there's an access door on the outside around back to get to the heating and cooling units. Not the kind of place you'd store things. Just a small cramped room, hardly big enough for a full-grown Ranthrr to stand upright in, what with all the equipment in there."

Seeker considered. "Let's check it anyway on the way out."

Krral shrugged. "Sure."

They went to the main door and let themselves out. The

night had become overcast and was very dark. Seeker could barely make out the even blacker bulk of the forest behind the house. The soft murmur of the wind and the occasional rustle and scramble of night hunters and their prey were all that could be heard. They circled around the building to the back, where Krral pointed out the door in the wall.

It took Krral only a moment to figure out the code. He touched it into the keypad and the door slid back. As it opened, a dark form lurched forward toward them.

With a curse of surprise, Krral leapt to one side and ripped out with his claws. But the form was not attacking. It was falling. It hit the ground on its face with a soft thud and lay there with an unnatural stillness.

"What the . . ." Krral muttered, looking down at the motionless shape that lay at his feet. It was a Ranthrr.

"Damurrl?" Seeker asked breathlessly.

Krral shook his head. "Wrong fur color." He knelt cautiously next to the body and turned it over. He cursed again. "Questioner, I'd like to introduce you to one of our star informants. One we've been hunting for. This is Drrulum. Or rather, this was Drrulum. Now it's just a chunk of rotting meat." He ran his hands over the corpse. "Not dead all that long. Maybe a couple of hours."

"Stabbed?" Seeker questioned.

Krral nodded in the dark. "Yeh. There's a dagger handle sticking out of his guts. About the same position as Doctor Frryml's. Another strange accident." He sat back. "No wonder Damurrl's not here. He's gone to ground someplace else after murdering Drrulum."

Seeker pondered for a moment. "Doesn't make sense. It would be much easier just to dump the body someplace else. Leaving it here where it can be directly tied to him is just too stupid for someone like Damurrl. It would have made more sense to murder Drrulum wherever he was hiding out. But to murder him somewhere else and then bring the body here, or to bring him here and then kill him, just doesn't ring true."

"Yeh. Makes sense. But if Damurrl didn't kill Drrulum, who did? And why would anyone else bring him here, dead or alive? We know he was working for Damurrl. We've got the Ranthaa's statement on that. Plus the number in Damurrl's commnet memory. What's more, this killing is just like Doctor

Frryml's, whose name is also in Damurrl's file. Not to mention the dagger connection with Branrrul and our suspicion that Damurrl's mixed up with this suicide thing somehow. Maybe it's all just a bunch of coincidences. But there sure are an awful lot of them in one lump, Questioner.''

''The Ranthaa never specifically said Drrulum worked for Damurrl, remember? She just hinted it. You supplied the name of Damurrl. And as for his name in the memory, that could be there for completely unrelated reasons. It could even be a plant. I agree that the connection with the daggers and with Frryml is pretty clear. But just because the murders are similar in style doesn't necessarily mean the same person or persons did both. Just that someone wants everyone to think that. However, the real question is, who would want us to think Damurrl had murdered both Frryml and Drrulum?''

''And maybe even Mraal. I'm not so sure I agree completely with what you're suggesting,'' Krral said hesitantly. ''But for the sake of argument I'll go with it for the moment.'' He paused. ''Got to admit this whole thing is getting more disturbing by the minute. It all just seems so . . . so damn un-Ranthlike, to quote the High Minister. Doesn't make any sense. I can guarantee you nothing even remotely like all this killing and dying has happened in at least a thousand years. Maybe even more. There's something very . . . unnerving about it, almost alien. So far I can't even imagine a motivation for all of it. Maybe that's only because of my limited, inside perspective. Maybe you already see things I'm blind to. I just don't know right now.'' He shuddered slightly. ''And I've got a bad feeling once I do know, I'm not going to like it one bit.

''In any case, it seems to me that it becomes more important than ever to talk with Damurrl. Murderer or not, he seems to be plunk right in the middle of this thing. Which brings up the point of exactly where he is.''

Seeker hesitated. ''Could he be dead, too?''

''Right now,'' Krral said with a growl, ''I would bet almost anybody could be dead. Seems to be a very catching condition. I'll put a check on all the morgues on Ranthar. But somehow, Questioner, I'm got a feeling that Damurrl is very much alive. In fact, if your line of reasoning is correct, the very fact that he's not here guarantees that he's still alive.''

''Then the question is, how do we find him before anybody

else finds him? If I am right, he's not hiding from us at all. He's hiding from whoever it is that killed Drrulum. And maybe Doctor Frryml as well.''

Krral considered. ''First thing is to pay a personal call on everyone on Damurrl's list. Since both Frryml and Drrulum were on it, it's just possible the others on it were involved in this mess in some way as well. We might get a lead there.''

''Or scare him even further into the underbrush. Haven't you got any other ways of finding things out, Krral? I'm not sure waving your claws under the noses of some twenty Ranth is going to bring Damurrl out of hiding.''

''O.K. I admit I've been a little heavy-handed so far. We'll try the subtle approach for a change. We stake out the most interesting places and see if there's any sign of Damurrl. That will take a lot longer, but I agree it's a lot less likely to make our prey bolt.'' He stood, looking down at Drrulum. ''Well, no more petty thievery for you, cubbo. You're one more Ranth who won't be around to take the immortality shot. Or pill or whatever. Since I doubt you're going anywhere, I'll send someone out to pick you up in the morning. Until then, enjoy the peaceful night.''

He turned from the body and the house and strode toward the dark forest. ''Come on then, Questioner. Let's get on it. It's going to take a while, so the sooner we get to it, the more likely we are to find Damurrl alive. Wouldn't that be a refreshing change?''

# III.

The first thing they checked was the passenger lists for the colony worlds. Since they didn't know which world Damurrl might run to, they had to check them all. Krral's high access rating made the job possible, but it was still tedious. Worse, it was fruitless. It appeared Damurrl had stayed on Ranthar.

Interestingly enough, Damurrl's file indicated he had spent his First Hundred on Ranth-urrl-Urthar. But the sample of the stone they had found among his Classical relics tested out to be unique to Ranth-urrl-Vynnur. Why, Krral wondered, would a Ranth who had spent his First Hundred on one world have a memento from a different one?

Even odder was the fact that the only names on Damurrl's personal commnet list that were scrambled were those of Drru-lum and Doctor Frryml. All the rest checked out as perfectly legitimate. Seeker suggested that perhaps someone other than Damurrl might have placed the two names there in order to confuse anyone investigating whatever was going on. In any case, it seemed another dead end.

The next task was to question all of Damurrl's associates, including his most recent mate. It was clear that he had told no one where he was going. The only clue they turned up was from Nasmaal, Damurrl's ex-mate.

Nasmaal was a Second Hundred Ranthaa with a very fetching

pale grey coat with dark grey paws and highlights above the eyes. Krral found her quite attractive. At first she seemed reluctant to talk about Damurrl, but after patient urging by Seeker through Krral, she opened up a little.

"We dissolved the mateship about two years ago," she finally admitted. "It just wasn't working any longer."

"Something changed?" Krral asked.

Nasmaal nodded slowly, frowning slightly. "Yes. Something. It's really very hard to explain. Damurrl always was involved with his Classical studies. A hobby, so to speak. A harmless enough one that gave us some interesting vacations to the southern landmass and a few to some very dull conferences. But other than that, he was a very lively and energetic Ranthrr. Fun to be with. His import business had done very well, as I'm sure you already know, and he had lots of extra credits to spend. A good chunk went to purchasing artifacts, but there was still plenty left over for other forms of entertainment." She smiled secretly.

Then she frowned and hesitated. "Then about three years ago, something happened. I'm not really sure what. I remember he came back from visiting a new find on one of the coastal islands off the southern landmass. A monument complex of some kind from the Classical times. Some great king or something."

"What changed?" Krral asked. "Try to remember as best you can. Just give me your impressions, even if they don't make much sense to you. They might mean something to me."

"Well . . . he was somewhat morose and very thoughtful. He would stand outside the house he has on that hill by the lakes and look off into the distance toward the lakes for hours. I asked him what was wrong so often he finally got tired of saying 'Nothing' and said something very strange. It was so odd, I can still remember it fairly well. 'That monument was to last forever and tell all Ranth to eternity of the greatness of the king who built it. But do you know, we can't even read his name or place him historically with any accuracy. The key sections are badly defaced, as if someone purposely destroyed them. Whoever he was, his monument stands and he is forgotten. No one even knows he ever lived.'

"I tried to cheer him up. I laughed and said that I felt sorry for those old Ranth because they wanted immortality so badly and couldn't have it. For us, it's just around the corner. There'd just been a story on the commnet about some very promising new research that was being conducted and I told him about it. He just looked at me, silent, for a long time. I felt very uncomfortable. Finally he smiled sadly and said, 'And so we build our own monuments. But they are so fragile, because they are constructed of nothing but promises, that they will not even stand one thousandth as long as that pile of stones down south. As soon as they are uttered, those words vanish, even as we will surely vanish.' He turned away from me and started looking out at the lakes again. Then he said, so softly I almost couldn't hear it, 'There is a desert, empty, waterless, where thought finally reaches its limits. There the mind hesitates in horror for an instant, uncertain where to go, unable to stay amidst the desolation. At that juncture, thought halts, and then moves on, down one path or another. Which path to take? Which path?'

"He . . . he never really cheered up. And then he started hanging around with those strange people." She shuddered in remembrance. "They gave me the creeps. So solemn and grave, never smiling or laughing. It wasn't long after that that we both began to realize we had no future together. I was the one who left. Damurrl was too kind, too sweet, even when he stopped being happy and cheerful, to cut me off.

"I still see him occasionally. The last time was, oh, perhaps six months ago. He's aged a lot in the last two years. Something seems to have gone out of him. He seems to be . . . oh, I don't know, he seems to be waiting for something."

When they had completed their questioning of Damurrl's friends and acquaintances, Seeker and Krral sat down to review all the information. "I think," Seeker finally said, "that we have been looking in all the wrong places."

"What makes you say that?" Krral asked. "We've been staking out all the places he usually goes. Ranth set up patterns in their lives and tend to stick to them. I've located more than one Ranthrr or Ranthaa by just hanging out where they usually hang out."

"I think Nasmaal gave us a hint that we should follow up," Seeker suggested. "And I think we need to go visit the Ranthaa in the museum to do so. She's the one who directed us to

Damurrl in the first place. I suspect that she knows him better than she let on at the time. From what I've gathered, Damurrl is more widely known in scholarly circles than we realized. And I'm positive she would have come across him more than once at conventions and conferences. Also, I want to ask her about Classical ruins on the southern landmass.''

Krral shrugged. ''I don't know what you're after, but we're not making much progress following usual methods, so let's try it. Nothing to lose and everything to gain.'' He paused, then added, ''As long as it doesn't involve going to Ranth-urrl-Vynnur, I'm all for it!''

''Yes,'' the Ranthaa said immediately, ''I've met Damurrl several times. Had more than one discussion with him. For a layman, he is remarkably knowledgeable. And on several occasions, he has loaned some of his artifacts to us for display or study. Indeed, I remember one conference when he gave a paper on . . .''

''Uh,'' Krral interrupted, ''yes, but have you seen him recently? Oh, say, in the last month or so?''

''Why, yes. Only a few weeks ago he came in and brought some things for us to borrow.'' She rummaged around on her desk. ''Yes, here it is. 'Two daggers of the Ranth Raquurrl style, late Classical; three medallions, early Classical; sacrificial bowl, pre-Classical from the northern landmass.' Yes. They will be on display at the beginning of the month in the Great Hall. Fine pieces. Very thoughtful of him.''

''Did he say anything about going away for a while?''

She thought. ''Not exactly. He said he'd pick up the pieces in six months or so. Hmmmmm. And yes, he wanted to see some files of ours.''

''Files?'' Krral asked, trying not to sound too eager. ''Do you remember which files?''

''Hmmmmmmm. Yes. I seem to recall . . . yes, they were the detailed dig reports on that monument that was discovered, oh, about four years ago down just off the southern landmass. I believe he had visited it once, just after the discovery. We thought it was Classical at first, you know, but we now believe it was pre-Classical. We are totally unable to place the king it commemorates.''

"This monument," Krral asked. "Can anyone go there? I mean, is it open to the public?"

"Not really. There isn't a fence around it or anything. But it's in a pretty remote valley in a very rugged area. Those islands are really the tops of a drowned mountain range that comes off the mainland. They rise very steeply from the sea, with almost no beach or flat area to speak of. Much of the terrain is virtually inaccessible except by foot, and the jungle down there is very dense."

"Could Damurrl get there?"

"Of course. There's a narrow cove where boats can land if the seas aren't running too high. And he's already visited the site once, so he wouldn't have any trouble finding it again. But there's no reason to go there right now. There's no digging going on. The place is deserted."

"That," Krral said solemnly, "is a very good reason to go there. May I see the file?"

The area was every bit as remote and inaccessible as the Ranthaa had indicated. Krral was exhausted by the three-day trek through dense jungle and rugged mountains and was very glad when he finally struggled into the clearing in which the monument stood. Seeker had found the trip fascinating, never having seen a jungle environment before. The dense and riotous life of the jungle had been almost overwhelming in its profusion.

They stood and stared in awe at the ruins in front of them. Most evident was a step pyramid, very narrow and steep, that towered up a good hundred feet, almost reaching the canopy made by the forest. The lowest step was a square perhaps four hundred feet on a side. Each step—there were seven in all—was faced with some sort of stone that had been richly carved. On the side to their left was a steep stairway of stone that led from the bottom to the top, where a small rectangular structure crowned the pyramid. The dig reports had called the structure a memorial temple. Scattered around the site, about twenty yards from the base of the pyramid, were smaller buildings, badly damaged and mostly just piles of rubble. Little excavation had taken place among them and no attempt at reconstruction had begun.

They walked around the pyramid. At the back side they found

a tent and a rather well-arranged campsite right at the edge of the clearing. Clearly someone was presently living there. Indeed, Krral noted that the klath pot was still warm and half full of klath.

"I think," Seeker suggested as they looked around the campsite, "that we have found our quarry. But I regret to inform you that to bring him to earth, we will have to leave earth."

"Make sense, Questioner," Krral replied grumpily. "I'm too tired for riddles."

"I mean," Seeker said with a chuckle, "that I believe Damurrl is to be found at the top of the monument. And that if we want to talk to him, that's where we'll have to go."

Krral groaned as he shrugged off the heavy pack he carried. "Can't we just wait down here for him? I could heat up the klath and when he returned we could just . . ."

"Krral, Damurrl knows we are here. He is up there where we can't see him, but where he definitely can see us. Now if we simply stay here waiting, he can always sneak down the opposite side of the pyramid from where we are, or he might just wait until night falls and slip away in the dark. I imagine he knows this region a lot better than we do and has already laid out escape routes for just such a situation as this. If he wishes to escape, that is. So, it seems logical . . ."

"Damn logic," Krral moaned. "I'm talking about my poor, sore legs and aching feet. I thought I was in pretty good shape, Questioner, but this trip has proven otherwise. All right, all right, I yield to your damn logic. Let me get my breath for a few seconds and it's up we go. But if we get up there and discover that rather than being in that temple, Damurrl has gone off to the store for more klath, I am going to be one angry Ranthrr."

The stairway was very steep and the steps quite narrow. Krral found he had to lean well forward and stay mostly on the balls of his feet to keep his balance. Naturally, in such a position his calf muscles took most of the weight and they were soon protesting by sending shooting pains through his legs. "I don't think I'll ever walk again," Krral grumbled. "How are we going to get back down? Jump?"

When they reached the top, Damurrl was standing in the temple doorway waiting for them. He had an amused smile on his face as he recognized Krral. "Ah, Operative Krral, I believe. I had been informed you were a resourceful Ranthrr, one of the old hunting type. The rumor proves to be true. Welcome to the monument of a king unknown, a Ranthrr who conquered everything there was to conquer and then lost it all to time and death.''

Damurrl turned and re-entered the temple. Krral followed, limping slightly, his legs still protesting the abuse of the steep climb.

The entire interior surface of the temple was covered with intricate carvings. Krral stared at them in wonder. Damurrl noticed his gaze and smiled sadly. ''His life, all carved out in imperishable stone. But notice the places here and there where someone has carefully chiseled away parts of the relief? Those spots were very carefully chosen. They contain his name symbol or the date symbols that would give anyone any hint as to who he was or when he lived. From what we know of this area and this time, he could be one of twenty or thirty minor kings. Or maybe one we don't even know of.'' He turned away from Krral and gestured sweepingly toward a statue which stood in the center of the temple. ''And there he himself stands in his full regalia. But carefully note the face. There is none. Someone has truly 'defaced' him. And on his regalia, all references, all symbols that might give a clue as to his time period, are likewise defaced. A very thorough job.''

''Damurrl,'' Krral said softly to his back, ''I found Drrulum at your place. He was murdered. Murdered with a dagger that was a perfect replica of yours.''

Damurrl stayed turned away, but Krral could see his shoulders sag. ''Ah, poor Drrulum. A rotten life and a rotten death to match. At my place? Any idea who did it?''

''I was hoping you might be able to help with that.''

Damurrl turned back slowly, a strange smile on his face. ''Not I, surely you know that. It could have been one of those fools from the Faction, but I doubt it.'' He sighed deeply. ''I fear I will not be of much help.''

''Your dagger,'' Krral began, ''is the one . . .''

''Yes, I know. I gave it to Doctor Frryml to have copies made by Branrrul. I lied to you about that. It was foolish. But I didn't realize how clever you are, Operative. Or perhaps it is your Questioner? Am I permitted to meet our visitor from Labyrinth? I'm really most anxious to do so.''

"Greetings, Damurrl," Seeker said, taking over from Krral.

"Ah," Damurrl sighed again. "How interesting. Krral changes quite dramatically when you are there, Questioner."

"So I have heard. What is this Faction you mentioned? And how might it be tied to Drrulum's death?"

"I don't think it is tied to Drrulum's death," Damurrl smiled slightly. "To Doctor Frryml's death, yes. But not to Drrulum's."

"To Doctor Frryml's? How?"

"Doctor Frryml failed. Obviously, or else neither you nor Krral would even be here. The Faction does not tolerate failure, and so poor Doctor Frryml had to die. Personally I despise their logic. A Ranthrr's death should be his own affair, not something any other Ranth should meddle in. But then the step from suicide to murder is but a short one."

Seeker gazed calmly at Damurrl. "The Faction murders those who fail. Murder is just a step from suicide. Is the Faction the Others that Master Grrul of the Lefthand Pathway spoke of?"

"Grrul? You've spoken to Grrul? How interesting. He calls us the Others? Amusing. We call him and his followers the Deluded Ones. Deluded because they think they can escape the Paradox by transcendence of some sort.

"But I wander into philosophy. Or, in Grrul's case, into religion. Yes and no to your question. The Faction is part of what Grrul was referring to as the Others. As a whole, we refer to ourselves, interestingly enough, as the Righthand Pathway. The Faction is just that, a faction, a part of our whole. And a rather foolish and troublesome part at that. Overly enthusiastic, shall we say?"

"Hmmmm. Master Grrul has a similar problem with his followers. One of them tried to kill Krral at the same time Doctor Frryml tried."

Damurrl laughed. "You and Krral are indeed an impressive pairing, Questioner. To escape two concerted efforts on your mutual lives."

"More than two attempts have been made," Seeker commented drily. "Was it the Faction that was behind Frryml's attempt?"

"No," Damurrl said, "that was a decision made by the leadership of the Righthand Pathway. The Faction only re-

acted—in an unauthorized fashion, I might add—to the failure.
I think they feared the weakness of Doctor Frryml and the
clearly well-earned reputation of your host, Krral. You could
trace us back through him much too directly."

"Have we found Mraal's murderers?"

Damurrl considered. "If you mean the Righthand Pathway,
the answer is no. If you refer to the Faction, the answer is that
I simply do not know. Possibly. But I tend to doubt it."

"Doubt it? Why?"

He shrugged. "Too many things, too subtle to really spell
out. It just doesn't seem like them. Besides, there are some
strange anomalies from what I understand. But I really can't
enlighten you on that score, I fear."

"If not Mraal's murderers, have we then found the source
of the wave of suicides?"

Damurrl smiled his strange smile again. "Indeed. That is
much, much closer to the mark, Questioner."

"Tell me of this Righthand Pathway, Damurrl."

He bowed his head slightly. "I am unworthy to expound the
doctrines, Questioner. I have never even been named one of
the Chosen for Solution. They do not really consider me one
of theirs. And perhaps I am not. Perhaps. I have given them
their dagger, true. But their use of it is their own. No, I cannot
tell you what you want to know." He paused and looked around
the temple. "And yet I can open it to you. Or better yet, this
temple can open it and give you a glimpse."

Damurrl stepped over to a narrow window in the right wall
of the temple and gestured for Seeker to follow. Side by side
they stood and gazed out the window. "What do you see,
Questioner?" Damurrl asked softly.

"Nothing much. The clearing, the trees. Up above, the sky.
The jungle cuts off any view down the mountain. The trees
are too high."

"And yet," Damurrl murmured, "you see all there is to
see. Out there in that jungle, Questioner, is life at its most
fecund. This jungle breathes life. Everywhere you cast your
gaze is life, growing, sprawling, crawling, stalking, leaping,
flying. Dying. For all that life means an equal amount of death.
Do you know what keeps this forest so filled with growth and
greenness? Death. The forest lives on its own constant death.
If it stopped dying, if trees ceased falling to the forest floor

and decaying, the thin soil would soon be depleted of its nourishing power and the forest would shrivel and die. Life on death, death for life. Amazing, isn't it?''

He turned back into the temple and pointed at the statue. ''But that is not nature. Nor is this entire complex natural. It did not grow here, part of the life-and-death cycle of the forest. It was placed here, gouged out of the riot of life.

''And what is it? It is a dead thing. Stone, stacked and carved stone. Oh, over the eons, it contributes its bit of life, slowly, slowly, as the very rock dissolves. And plants lodge in the cracks between the stones where rotten matter has found a home and provides nourishment. But the monument itself is inert, lifeless.

''Yet it is meant to commemorate life, even to commemorate life eternal. Immortality, Questioner, that is what this monument is about. Built here by a mighty king to stand forever in testimony of his greatness and power. A statement to all ages to bow down before such awesome majesty, a statement meant to cow, to daunt, to wring all the anguish of despair from all future Ranth who could never hope to attain such glory and deathless fame.''

He paused and walked over to the statue. Seeker followed. ''And what,'' he said softly as if to himself, ''has it become? Built by how many hundreds or thousands at what price of pain and toil, what is it now? Now that one chisel has carefully defaced it? What is it?''

Damurrl turned to Seeker. In his right hand he held the original sacrificial knife they had viewed in his home. He smiled sadly, his eyes filled with a strange, questioning light. ''What is it now?'' he repeated in a gentle murmur.

''Since you do not, cannot, answer, I will tell you. It is a living monument to the Paradox. Ah, Questioner, the futility! Think of it! All this''—he gestured with the dagger—''all this planning and labor, all this incredible ego, for nothing! His name is not even known! Nothing is left but an empty gesture!

''This is what it is to be Ranth, Questioner! An empty gesture! A swift flash of intense light in the dark of the infinite universe. Blinding the eye with glory for an instant, then gone, dispersing into endless night in all directions, an invisible, undetectable, entropy death.''

He laughed bitterly. ''We will be immortal, they tell us. We will soon live forever. The answer is just around the corner. Those are the temples we build, Questioner. They are temples of words, of promises to ourselves that we cannot keep. They do not last even as long as this monument, lost in the jungle for eons, defaced and indecipherable, has lasted. No sooner are our promises of immortality uttered than they are called back. No, not quite yet. But soon, so soon."

Damurrl laughed again, the bitterness replaced by a weary defeat. "When I saw this place, I knew I had arrived somewhere I had never been before, somewhere I had never even known existed. I had come to a place, a vast and waterless desert that stretches off in all directions and which is without end. A desert which, once entered, can never be left again.

"There is no hope there, though some pretend to find it. And following some trace they believe will lead them once again to green and happy lands, hoping, they wander on and on until they die, hoping still."

His voice had dropped to the merest whisper. "When the mind reaches that place and discovers it is in the desert, it hesitates for a moment. In that moment thought finds either hope or knows utterest despair. Those who despair see no reason to wander endlessly. They know all traces are false, all monuments futile and destined to be defaced, all promises hollow and meaningless. There is only one answer, one last act of defiance." He held up the knife and looked at the curve of its blade, his mouth curving to match it. "This," he murmured. "This."

His eyes focused slowly on Seeker's once more. "I have long known that place in the desert, Questioner. Known it on my own with no one from the Righthand Pathway to guide me. But you should seek them out. Go to the city of Ranmaasr on the northern landmass. Ask for Vururrl. Give my name. He will be able to tell you all that you wish to know about the Righthand Pathway and the suicides." His eyes dropped again to the blade in his hand.

"And what will you do, Damurrl?" Seeker asked gently.

Damurrl raised startled eyes. "What? Ah, yes, what will I do?" He chuckled slightly, an empty sound that rang strangely in the temple. "I will stay here. Yes. I will stay here forever. Although my thoughts will escape this desert, Questioner. They will escape in the only way possible."

Seeker nodded slowly. "I think I understand."

"Perhaps. Yes, perhaps, someone who has been on Labyrinth can understand the Paradox and what it means. But then, perhaps not. For you survived, didn't you? And so you still stand in the desert, you still stand at that crossroads where thought comes to a halt and gazes about in utter dismay. So perhaps you do not understand at all."

"I did not survive Labyrinth because I had hope, Damurrl," Seeker said softly. Then the Questioner turned away. *Time to leave, Krral,* it said to its host. *There is no reason to stay any longer.*

# IV.

❧❦❧

Krral accessed a private transportation pod for the journey to the northern landmass and the city of Ranmaasr. All the way there, he sat silent and thoughtful, working on shaping and sharpening his claws with a special set of tools he took from a small pouch on his harness. Half in respect for its host's contemplative mood, half because it had many questions of its own to work through, Seeker was as silent as Krral.

Just before they reached their destination, Krral gave his claws a critical look, nodded with satisfaction, and put away his tools. Then he reached out to activate the datanet that was built into the pod. "Ranmaasr, background," he touched into the keypad.

The data appeared almost instantly. Ranmaasr, it turned out, was a very ancient place. The present city was built on the ruins of no less than fifteen previous cities. The lowest level so far explored indicated that the city had originally been a ceremonial center in early pre-Dynastic times. In all likelihood, the first settlements on the spot dated back to Neolithic times.

That information absorbed, Krral asked for Vururrl's file. Vururrl, it turned out, was a Third Hundred Ranthrr who had served his First Hundred on Vynnur. His Second Hundred had been spent in a rather undistinguished career with several administrative branches of governmental agencies on both the northern and southern landmasses. For the last thirty years, he had been living quietly in Ranmaasr. There was no indication anywhere in his record that he had ever run afoul of any law.

Krral growled softly as he read the file. "Too damn ordinary! Nothing. Not even a drunken spree when he was on Vynnur. It's got to be a faked file, Questioner. Or else this Vururrl is the dullest Ranthrr that ever drew breath. Huh. Look at this. A very steady, very slow, very expected rise within the bureaucratic ranks. Never did one outstanding thing. Never made any mistakes. Never did anything!" In disgust, he blanked the screen. "And I used to have faith in those damn files! I wonder how many have been tampered with?"

"I assume at least the address is correct," Seeker commented mildly. "Ranmaasr seems to be a small city, so it shouldn't be hard to find him."

"Oh, we'll find him," Krral promised. Then he snorted. "Huh. I just hope I can keep my eyes open while we're questioning him!"

The pod left them near the center of Ranmaasr. They checked a city map, which was on display at the transportation center, and quickly located Vururrl's residence. Krral nodded thoughtfully. "Interesting. Right at the very outskirts of the city. Almost in the countryside. It looks like a rather out-of-the-way place for a Third Hundred Ranthrr to live." He pointed to the map. "See? Those symbols indicate that most of the buildings in the area are automated warehouses. Not many Ranth live around there. That's definitely odd."

"Why odd?" Seeker asked. "As I remember, Damurrl's house was quite isolated."

Krral scratched his head. "That was different. Damurrl's house was in a place of rare beauty. A natural setting like those we once hunted in. That kind of thing draws many Ranth during their last Hundred. But generally, Third Hundred Ranth like to be around other Ranth. Vururrl's living in a warehouse district is hardly living in a place of beauty. Plus there are no Ranth around. It just seems doubly odd, that's all. Maybe he really is as dull as his file indicates."

They took ground transportation to a spot about a half-mile from where Vururrl lived and then walked the rest of the way. Krral had been correct. The area was one of large buildings, closed and silent. There were no Ranth anywhere to be seen on the streets.

When they arrived at Vururrl's address, Krral became very thoughtful. It was another of the large, still warehouse buildings. Standing across the street from the building, he studied it. "I don't like this, Questioner. Too isolated. No one around. The whole thing smells like a trap."

"I agree," Seeker said. "But a trap is only set when one knows the quarry is about. Do you think Vururrl is aware we're looking for him? Perhaps they got into the file and substituted this address for the real one?"

"Nothing would surprise me any more," Krral growled, looking about warily. "But we're about as obvious standing here as a Brranth on a holiday cruise. Even if they didn't know we were coming, they sure must know we're here by now." He shrugged. "Best thing might be to just go with it."

Acting on his own suggestion, Krral immediately crossed the street and touched the commnet button on the door of the building. The screen stayed blank, but a voice answered instantly. "Yes? Who is it?"

"At least it's not a robot," Krral muttered softly under his breath. "Open up," he demanded loudly. "Operative Krral of the Service to see Vururrl. Priority One. Check it if you want."

"No need." The was a click and the door swung inward. "Come in, Operative Krral of the Service. And welcome."

Immediately inside the door was an anteroom where two large Ranthrr, obviously guards, stood awaiting Krral. They nodded as he entered and then gestured for him to follow. Without looking back, they moved to a door on the right and passed through. All senses at full alert, Krral followed.

They briskly walked single file down a long, empty corridor to a second door. One of the Ranthrr opened the door and nodded for Krral to enter. They both stepped back from the door to give Krral plenty of space. *I guess they've heard about your temper,* Seeker commented drily. Krral just growled silently in response.

Inside the door was a very attractive Ranthaa seated at a desk. She looked up as Krral entered and gave him a cool, appraising glance. "Master Vururrl will see you in just a moment," she said, her voice formal, but vibrant with warm undertones. "Please have a seat."

Krral looked around and realized he was in a very luxurious office. With a shrug, he stepped over and sat in a soft chair covered with a thick, beautifully woven fabric. Although it was abstract, Krral could swear the design included the shapes of sacrificial daggers in it. He sat back, appearing to be relaxed, but his body was poised for instant action. He allowed his eyes to wander around the room, checking the location of items, the placing of doors, and most of all, the attractive Ranthaa.

In less than five minutes, a door opened behind the Ranthaa and a rather small, nondescript Ranthrr, his fur streaked with grey, appeared in the doorway. He cast an uncertain look at the secretary, as if seeking confirmation. She nodded at Krral. Then he came forward, a broad smile on his face. "Ah, Operative Krral! At last we meet. I knew we would. Some of them said you'd never get this far. But I knew, I knew!" He chuckled with delight and winked at Krral. "You've won me a very good wager, sir! I am indebted to you. Now, will you do me the honor of stepping into my office? I am, as I'm sure you have already surmised, Vururrl. I imagine we have a great deal to discuss. And of course I am most curious to make the acquaintance of your Questioner."

Rather mystified, but still fully alert, Krral rose with one fluid movement and followed Vururrl into his office. Once inside, Vururrl motioned Krral to a comfortable chair and then pulled up another one himself. "Could sit behind that stupid desk and act official," he muttered with a slight smile, "but somehow I think you wouldn't be very impressed. Hopefully we are both beyond such foolish pretense."

When they were seated, Vururrl graced Krral with another huge smile and said, "So, how much do you already know and what more would you like to know?"

"I know that the organization you 'represent,' assuming that is the right word, is responsible for the death of Doctor Frryml, Drrulum, and probably the death of all the other Ranth who have had 'accidents' with daggers, for several attempts on my life, and most likely for the rash of suicides in recent years."

Vururrl sighed. "Basically correct. Though Doctor Frryml and most of the other 'accidents' are the work of a group we call the Faction, a rather fanatic subgroup over which the main group seems to have relatively little control.

"But let me be more specific. Yes, we were behind the first

attempt on your life. We hoped to abort the transfer of the Questioner to your mind as host. Our hope was the transfer would be aborted and that you would survive. I know that seems hard to believe now, but it is true.

"When Doctor Frryml failed so miserably, the Faction stepped in and punished him." He shrugged. "It was regrettable, but believe it or not, it was not totally out of line with Frryml's own wishes. He has long begged to be Chosen for Solution. Though I, for one, believe very firmly that Solution can only be achieved through the exercise of one's own will and act, not through that of others. I still maintain that suicide and murder, even murder of one who intends suicide, are radically different things. No Ranth has a right to share in the death of any other. There can be no sharing of death."

He paused for a moment, as if considering. "Hmmmmm. But as to the death of Drrulum, I was not even aware he was dead. I fear you will have to search elsewhere for those guilty of that crime. We had no share in it."

"What is this Solution and this Chosen business?" Krral asked. "We've heard the term several times now."

"'We'? Ah, yes, of course! You and the Questioner. Well, the Solution refers to our way out of the Paradox. And Chosen is, well, is the name we give those who are chosen to participate in a group Solution. We try to keep it neat and organized. No reason for it to be sloppy and painful. No reason at all. Do it with dignity is my feeling."

"Then," Seeker said through Krral, "Solution is suicide?"

"Indeed," Vururrl replied, looking with curious fascination at Krral. "How interesting. Indeed, Solution is suicide. Done in a group, carefully controlled and supervised. Each of the Chosen takes a draught of a pain-relieving drug, a mild soporific that gives a sense of general well-being. Then they all take their daggers, hold them in the proper position, and at the command, thrust them home. Death is almost instantaneous since the heart is burst by the blade."

Krral mused. "Suicide is the Solution. What is being solved?"

Vururrl smiled gently. "Life," he said simply. "The pain of living, the Paradox of despair."

"Despair? Pain? What are you talking about? We are Ranth! There is no pain or despair in our lives." Krral's tone was mild, and even Vururrl could sense the overtones of unsureness.

He nodded. "Indeed, indeed, so goes the common wisdom. And why do Ranth have no despair, no pain? No pain because we have outlawed it by our advanced medical science. All pain, all real pain, is banished. No one hungers, no one need suffer. There is food for everyone and medicines for every disease.

"Or, rather, for almost every disease. There is one we still have not conquered."

Krral looked at the grey-furred Ranthrr and said softly, "Death? You mean death."

Vururrl nodded again. "Death. Or perhaps, to put it another way, life. For death is nothing in itself. It is living that is painful."

"I don't understand," Krral said quietly, his tone puzzled and disturbed. "Damurrl said similar things. Things that seemed foolish to me at the time. But the more I think about them, the more I wonder. How can you fear death when a cure for it is just around the corner? The other day there was a report . . ."

Vururrl laughed. "Another report. Shall I tell you what it said? Something like this. 'A new line of research has opened exciting possibilities in the search for the immortality drug.' Don't look surprised! Think! How many times in your own, what, hundred and twenty, thirty, years have you heard that same report? And how many times in my three hundred and twenty-three years have I heard it?

"Krral, Krral, it's a lie! A fabrication! Oh, yes, there is research being conducted. But it is the same research over and over again. Long, long ago progress ceased being made. There is no immortality drug. There never will be. All paths that have been tried have led to the same dead end. Ranth live to be three hundred plus. They will never live any longer."

In a sudden burst of energy, Vururrl rose from his chair and began pacing back and forth as he spoke. "The lie has been told too often. The hope been disappointed too many times. The myth of immortality being just around the corner is wearing thin.

"And when that myth dies, what happens to all the Ranth have accomplished? What happens to the glory of our race? Hah!" He snapped his fingers. "It becomes a mere finger-snap of time, a brief instant that passes and disappears! Life, Krral, our glorious life, is meaningless!''

He sat down suddenly again and fixed Krral with burning eyes. ''If life is meaningless, if life is nothing but a Paradox, then it is life that is the disease and not death! Do you understand? We have been spending all our time trying to cure the wrong thing!'' He chuckled. ''If life is nothing but an empty Paradox, a situation from which there is no meaningful exit, then it is the disease and death must be the cure!''

He laughed heartily at the expression on Krral's face. ''Ah, ah, Krral! How many times have I seen that expression on the faces of Ranth! It is always the same when they realize the truth! All those years of believing suddenly swept away. Oh, they fight it, deny it, but slowly, slowly it creeps into their souls, into the very deepest silence of their hearts. Life is absurd, it comes from nowhere and goes to nowhere. A futile struggle against inevitable defeat. Why? Why? If it has no meaning, if there is no cosmic significance, why? Better to end it, to cure it, to return it to the nowhere it sprang from as soon as possible.

''Shall I tell you what would have been best for us as a race and as individuals? Never to have been born! But since we cannot accomplish that, shall I tell you what is next best? To die as swiftly as one can!''

Krral found himself unable to respond, so Seeker took over. ''Then these mass suicides, they are by Ranth who agree with your analysis of the situation?''

''How formal!'' Vururrl chuckled. ''Dear me, 'analysis of the situation.' I am not speaking of analysis, Questioner. I am speaking of what the mind discovers when it reaches that place where nothing makes sense any longer, that desert in the mind and soul of a Ranth when all thought must hesitate before the blatant absurdity of the Paradox.

''From that point, only two courses are open. The first is that chosen by Grrul and his fools. One has lost one hope, one belief, so one finds another. One *believes* one can transcend the Paradox without dying. But that belief is just as hollow as the others, for it is a belief that life is wellness and death is sickness. Sooner or later it must come face to face with death, unavoidable death, and then it must realize the futility of its claims. I've often wondered what Grrul will say with his last breath. I'm sure it will be either a final affirmation of foolish belief, a last grand gesture of futility, or it will be a curse against the disease of life and his own blindness.

"The other choice is our choice. To end this foolishness, this pain, this anxiety, this disease. A small draught. A quick thrust. And the disease is cured." Vururrl shrugged. "It is so simple, really, once one gets past the first sense of fear. Life is a very powerful disease and surrounds itself with many protections. But once they are breached by doubt, the end is only a matter of time. The cure is in Krral's mind now. It is in the silence of his heart. The rest is inevitable."

Krral shook his head slowly. "I'm not so sure, Vururrl. Only two choices? I'm not so sure. But in any case, then, you are the source of the suicides?"

Vururrl shrugged. "The source? Hardly. Life is the source of death. I am merely the means of administering it. The carrier of the cure, so to speak."

"And," Krral asked, his voice suddenly very soft, "did you cure Mraal as well?"

Vururrl shook his head firmly. "No. Neither I nor the Faction are responsible for the death, or rather, the murder of Mraal. That should be obvious to you, Krral."

Krral raised one eyebrow. "Obvious? How obvious?"

The old Ranthrr sighed. "We certainly could have killed her; that's not what I mean. But think of the Questioner she was host to, Krral. Think of where it was found. There is no way we could have accomplished that. We simply haven't the capacity. No, Mraal is not on our conscience. You must look elsewhere."

Krral frowned and sat silently for several moments. "I must report this, you know. My assignment, direct from High Minister Shyrrl himself, was to find the source of the growing number of suicides. The Ministry is very concerned."

Vururrl laughed. "And well might they be! For the growing number of those who seek and are Chosen for Solution gives the lie to all the Ministry's reassurances that immortality is just down the next trail we follow. What do you suppose will happen when all Ranth everywhere come to see the truth?" He laughed again. "By comparison to us, the danger represented by the Emperor and all his Furmorian mercenaries was a mere nuisance."

He nodded as he stood. "Yes, yes, you must make your report. No attempts will be made to stop you any longer. Even the Faction sees the wisdom of that."

He held out his hand as Krral also stood. "High Minister Shyrrl will doubtless act against us. He has wanted to for a long time. Your report will allow him to go to the Supreme Committee and demand action. They will agree. They must. But it does not matter. It is too late. The Righthand Pathway is filled with those seeking Solution. And it will grow and grow as more and more see the truth. We cannot be stopped. Halted for a moment, perhaps. But not stopped." He took Krral's hand in both of his. "Good hunting to you, Krral. When you wish to speak to me again, and I am sure you will, just put the word out and someone will come to bring you to me. I like you. I like your spirit and your hunting instinct. I will be happy to welcome you into the Righthand Pathway."

"Don't wait up nights," Krral growled and stalked from the office. He didn't even bother to look at the Ranthaa. Dead females had never interested him.

"Well, Questioner," he finally said as they left the building and strode away down the street, "that much of our search is complete."

"Yes," Seeker responded thoughtfully. "That much."

# PART FOUR

❧ ❦ ❧

*The Vigil of the Mind*

# I.

High Minister Shrryl sat back and smiled broadly. He nodded his head vigorously. "Yes, yes, Operative Krral, an excellent report! You've managed to uncover two sources of dangerous influence. Both the followers of Master Grrul and those of Vururrl. Hmmmm, hmmmm, yes, that latter group is especially of grave concern for the Ministry since they are clearly the ones behind all the suicides and all the murders. Yes, yes. Well done. Please thank the Questioner who aided you in this task. Although I imagine it's already gone now that the job is finished. I will personally see that a commendation is entered into your record."

"Thank you, sir," Krral said with a frown, "but the problem is that . . ."

Shrryl wasn't even listening. He was staring off into space and talking softly to himself. "Now I will be able to go before the Supreme Committee, with well-documented proof, and ask for the power to act against this . . . this suicide cult. They are very dangerous, very dangerous indeed. They strike right at the very roots of our system, at the very roots of what it means to be Ranth. We cannot, must not, hesitate to sweep them away!" His gaze suddenly focused on Krral and an expression of annoyed surprise flashed across his features. "Ah, Operative Krral, um, yes, what are you still doing here?"

Krral's frown deepened. "Sir, I need your permission to gain access to certain files in order to . . ."

"Access? Files? What on Ranthar for? The investigation is over, Krral. You've found out all there is to find out. Your report is wonderfully complete and gives me everything I had hoped for. A well-done job. But now it's complete. There's no need to look at any files."

Krral shook his head firmly. "It's hardly complete, High Minister. I still haven't found out who murdered Mraal."

Shrryl looked exasperated. "Of course you have! It's obvious that Vururrl and his crew are responsible. And believe me, they'll pay dearly for that crime! Your mate will be fully revenged, Krral!"

Krral's expression became stubborn. "I don't believe that either Vururrl or the Faction killed Mraal. In addition to Vururrl's own denial, I've studied Mraal's wounds. The Faction always kills with one thrust through the ribs and upward into the heart. The suicides are always from the left side into the heart, again, a single thrust. Mraal was murdered with three thrusts. That doesn't fit the pattern."

Shrryl seemed flustered. "But . . . that's hardly evidence! I mean, the obvious connection is the murder weapon, the sacrificial dagger, not the number of stabs. No, no, I cannot agree, Krral. It is clear that the murderers of Operative Mraal were followers of the Righthand Pathway."

"And then there's the issue of the Questioner," Krral continued, ignoring the High Minister's interruption. "If the Questioner had realized in time that Mraal was being murdered, and that in the best interests of its mission it should abandon its host, it might have been able to disengage and return to its ship."

"Well, yes, and clearly that is what happened. Why, you've read the report yourself. It was found in an escape capsule or something like that. Something happened to its ship and it had to eject. Hmmmm, yes, something like that."

Krral shook his head. "Remember I used the words 'might have been able to disengage.' Generally, that is impossible without a lot of time to prepare. Even then, I'm not sure it's possible except under very special circumstances. So the whole story seems a bit strained. All the evidence indicates that Mraal was surprised, High Commissioner. She was surprised and put up a good struggle. The odds are high that in such a case, if it is indeed as it appears, the Questioner would not have had an adequate opportunity to prepare for disengagement.

"And then there's another problem that's even more difficult to resolve." Krral paused and gave Shrryl a long, considering look. "Much more difficult."

"Problem?" Shrryl's voice rose slightly, his exasperation turning to clear annoyance. "What do you mean?"

"The report, sir, can't be correct. The Questioner couldn't have been found in an escape module after the mysterious explosion of its ship."

"What? Why not?"

"Because those ships don't have escape modules."

Shrryl stared blankly at Krral. Krral smiled slightly, then continued. "And then there's the question of exactly what happened to the Questioner's ship. Could it have been destroyed by some sort of an internal malfunction? Or perhaps a stray meteor may have struck it?

"Neither is very likely. Those ships are so highly sophisticated that they're simple and almost malfunction-free. They have a protection screen against meteors. And besides, they always place themselves in orbits which are as safe as possible. About the only way one of them could be destroyed in such a sudden and cataclysmic manner would be if they were attacked with a thermonuclear device. A missile, say.

"Quite simply, High Minister, the Righthand Pathway has no access to either missiles to destroy a Questioner's ship, or to escape modules to put a Questioner's body in. The conclusion is obvious enough." Krral fell silent and sat staring at the High Minister.

For several moments, Shrryl simply gazed vaguely into space. Then he shook himself and turned his eyes on Krral. The expression in them was hard and hostile. "Uh, interesting ideas, Operative Krral. Interesting, but I'm not too sure they hold water. We don't know yet precisely how far into the government the followers of the Righthand Pathway have penetrated. Perhaps it is even further than I had estimated. In fact, your suggestions would indicate it was far indeed. Hmmmmm, yes, yes. Good evidence in a way. I will use your suggestions to convince the Supreme Committee of the immediate danger of this group to governmental security as well. Yes."

He smiled coldly. "But there is no need for you to investigate any further, Krral. Your assignment is terminated. I'm lifting your Status One access as of now. Thank you and goodbye." He turned brusquely from Krral in dismissal and began to work with his datanet, ignoring the other Ranthrr as if he had ceased to exist.

Krral stood slowly and walked to the door of High Minister Shrryl's office. When he reached the door, he paused and turned back. His voice was soft, but penetrating. From the sudden stiffening of Shrryl's shoulders, he knew the High Minister heard him. "The official investigation may be over, Shrryl. But my personal investigation isn't. I claim Blood Right for my mate. And I'll have it. No matter who murdered her, I'll find them and take my Right. Good day." He left.

The High Minister sat for some time, staring sightlessly at his datanet screen as he considered the situation. Then he switched his commnet on and touched in a series of numbers and a Level A Security Code. "Yes?" said a disembodied voice. The screen stayed blank.

Shrryl sat silent for a moment, gazing thoughtfully at the empty screen. Then he uttered one word. "Krral."

"Yes," came the answer. "Right away."

Krral sat in his office and worked at his datanet. Seeker was surprised when he entered a Status One code and it was acknowledged. "I thought Shrryl was taking it away?"

The Ranthrr grunted. "He did. Instantly. But I expected that to happen, so I created a second persona, Operative Rralk, and shared my Status One with him. Officially, he's working on the case with me. Eventually, the file will be rejected when the system realizes Rralk is a phony. Maybe when it comes time to pay him or something. But until then, I'm the only one who knows the access codes to Rralk's files, so there's no way Shrryl can rub it out."

Seeker chuckled. "Very clever. And precisely what are we looking for?"

Krral shook his head. "Damned if I know. I'm starting with Shrryl's file. There seem to be some odd bends in the system around his file, but . . . ah, there it is." The data came up on the screen. Krral stared at it.

"Hmmmm, hmmmm. Notice anything interesting?"

Seeker considered. "Yes. It appears High Minister Shrryl spent his First Hundred on Vynnur. Just like Damurrl."

"And like Drrulum and like Vururrl. I checked. All from Vynnur. And even more interesting, all of them were there at overlapping times."

He sat back and stared off into space. "Questioner," he finally said, "what kind of place would bring you face to face with this Paradox both Grrul and Vururrl talk about?"

Seeker considered. "Most likely a place where death is sudden and random. A place where you can die horribly and fruitlessly. Like Grrul's mate. Here on Ranthar things are too easy. It's simple to hide from the fact of death because you're all so sure of immortality. Even here, though, as Damurrl discovered, mortality makes its statements."

Krral nodded slowly. "Makes sense. Vynnur and Gobnar are probably two of the most hostile environments of all the Ranth colony worlds. Urthar's not exactly a paradise either, but it's not as bad as those other two. Gobnar gave birth to the Lefthand Pathway. Could it be that Vynnur gave birth to the Righthand Pathway?"

"It seems possible. And if so, then we have to ask what the relationship between those who would have been there at the time of its birth might be."

"Yes," Krral said. "I remember Urmaal very well." He was silent again for a few moments. "If Shrryl and Vururrl knew each other the way Grrul and Urmaal did, and something happened between them, again like Snurrl happened between Grrul and Urmaal, we might have the makings of a very nasty situation."

Seeker agreed. "Which might explain the very evident glee with which Shrryl looks forward to crushing the Righthand Pathway and Vururrl."

"You noticed that too, eh? He was practically frothing at the mouth to get at them! How could we find out?"

"Damurrl?" Seeker suggested.

Krral nodded slowly. "Damurrl. If he's still alive."

Seeker gave a small laugh. "Somehow I'm sure he is. I think Damurrl enjoys contemplating suicide a lot more than committing it. It gives him good company. And why part from good company?"

\* \* \*

Damurrl was still at the temple, still meditating on the futility of life, still running wondering fingers over the places where the ancient king's name had been chiseled from immortality.

"Shrryl and Vururrl? Ah, your hunting instincts are very keen, Krral. Very keen. To join the two of them and me. How did you connect me with them?"

"The memento in your home. Your file says you spent your First Hundred elsewhere, but the memento says Vynnur. I trust mementos more than files."

Damurrl chuckled. "Indeed. A wise decision. Though I am annoyed, since it cost me a good deal to get that file changed." He paused and leaned back against the wall of the temple, gazing up toward the ceiling. "Shrryl and Vururrl and Damurrl. Ah, that does bring back memories. And, of course, poor, stupid Drrulum.

"Where to begin? On Vynnur, obviously. The three of us were practically littermates. When the time came, we chose Vynnur because it was one of the few colony worlds we could be sure they would post all of us to without any questions. No one else wanted to go there! So three volunteers had their choice.

"We went and were inseparable. We worked together, played together, even had mates together! A harsh world, Vynnur, but when one has the close companionship of littermates everything seems easier."

He paused for a long time, lost in the past. Eventually he came back from his wanderings and began his narration again. "But, of course, on a place like Vynnur, happiness is a fragile, tenuous thing. We had mates, the three of us, and we all went out on the surface, for a lark, really, to explore a bit.

"Vynnur is cold. Incredibly cold. On the nightside, the temperature gets down very close to Absolute Zero. But Vynnur is also incredibly beautiful. The ice takes fantastic forms and the colors are almost beyond belief. Overall it's pinkish, but the subtle tones of red and green and yellow are stunning. And then there are the ice volcanoes. Unbelievable."

His gaze became sad and weary, his shoulders slumped, even his fur seemed to droop. "Our vehicle broke down. Shrryl and I volunteered to go for help. It was a foolhardy thing to do. But there was no real alternative. Vururrl and our mates stayed behind in the relative safety of the vehicle's cabin. They should have been all right. We were the ones in danger.

"We managed to find our way to a station and get help. I still don't know how we did it. When we got back to the vehicle something had gone wrong. Some system had failed or something, I don't know. Only Vururrl was still alive, though barely. The others, our mates, were dead. Dead."

Damurrl sighed deeply and rose. He went over to the narrow window and gazed out. Then he turned back to Krral. "It was one of those things that happen in places like Vynnur." He shrugged. "I accepted it. But Shrryl couldn't. He was convinced Vururrl was to blame for the deaths of our mates. *We* had managed to stumble across that hostile, desolate landscape and find help. *He* had failed to keep everyone alive in a fairly safe environment. Shrryl couldn't forgive that or forget it.

"Naturally, our friendship dissolved after that. I remained on passably good terms with both Shrryl and Vururrl, even after we came back to Ranthar. But they hated each other."

"Where does Drrulum fit in?" Krral asked.

Damurrl laughed. "Poor, stupid Drrulum came to Vynnur about halfway through our service. He sort of hung around the outskirts of our group. There was no way he could gain entrance to such a tight relationship, but he loved us nonetheless. Then when the breakup occurred, he tried to become close friends with each of us individually. We all tolerated him, used him to do small favors, things like that. A fool, but often a useful one. The same pattern continued here on Ranthar."

Krral perked up at that. "Do you mean to say that Drrulum worked for Shrryl as well as for you?"

Damurrl nodded. "Of course. And for Vururrl too."

"Ah," Krral mused, digesting the information, "I see. Do you think . . . that Drrulum was capable of killing for one of you?"

The question disturbed Damurrl. "Killing? For one of us?" He paused. "No. No, I don't believe Drrulum was capable of killing for anybody. He was basically a coward."

Krral considered. "I tend to agree. So it had to be someone else, then. Someone who would be able to kill. Someone who was actually good at it."

Damurrl looked puzzled. "What are you talking about?"

Krral smiled bitterly. "The original search is over, Damurrl. I'm no longer working on High Minister Shrryl's assignment to discover the source of the suicides. Now I'm on my own quest. I'm looking for the murderer of Mraal. I have a Blood Right to work out here."

The other Ranthrr nodded solemnly. "I understand. I'm sorry that I can't do any more to help you, but that's honestly all I have to tell."

"You've helped me more than you know, Damurrl," Krral said as he rose to leave. "You've cleared up several things that didn't seem to make any sense. And provided a couple of connections I had missed. Enjoy your life of suicide."

Their return to Krral's residence was late at night. It was raining lightly and the streets were deserted. Krral seemed unusually preoccupied, so the Questioner left him to think and took over many of his sense perceptions in order to allow the Ranthrr to devote more of his energy to his internal contemplations.

Krral was still living in the same accommodations he and Mraal had shared. As a result, the place was bigger than one Ranth needed. But Krral had been so busy with his investigations that he had not had time to arrange a change of residence.

The front entrance of his building was covered by a slight overhang. As they were about to enter, something set off alarms in Seeker's mind. The Questioner halted Krral. "Krral, please take a look at that."

The Ranthrr came out of his thoughtful fog on full alert. "What?" Seeker indicated a small spot of water near the front door. "Water? What of it? It's raining."

"Yes. But it's raining very gently. No wind or anything to blow water this close to the door. The overhang should keep all water that might drip much further out."

Krral nodded slowly. "Right. I'm very happy I am host to a Questioner who comes from a hunting species. Any thoughts on where the water might come from? Or what it means?"

Seeker considered. "Well, if we were still in the middle of the investigation, I'd be worried about the Faction. That water could very well have come from a Ranth who let itself in through the door and was waiting inside with a dagger. But the investigation is over and the Faction is no longer a problem.

So perhaps the water comes from a Ranth who let itself in through the door and is waiting inside . . ."

Krral finished the sentence. "With a dagger. But not from the Faction or from Vururrl or Grrul. This Ranth is from whoever the real murderer of Mraal is." Krral flicked out his claws. "You may be wrong, Questioner. The drops may have come from some random breeze that just blew it there." His voice was a throaty purr, filled with repressed excitement. "But I sincerely hope you are right."

"Krral, I know what you're thinking. But maybe it's more than one Ranth. Wouldn't the best thing be to call for support? Call for help from the Service or something?"

"And what," Krral responded softly, "if those behind the door are *from* the Service?" That stopped Seeker. "No, Questioner, I'll handle this one alone. As I have all the others. My Blood Right is involved, and that's how it has to be."

Krral turned abruptly from the front door and went around to the left side of the building. "But at the same time, I don't intend to walk into a trap like a stupid fool. We'll go in the back way."

"I didn't know there was a back way," Seeker commented.

The Ranthrr chuckled quietly. "There isn't. At least, there isn't supposed to be. But I don't like a den with only one way in and out. So I devised another one. Through the heating and power tunnels."

Halfway down the street that ran along the side of Krral's building, they came to a metal door at the base of the wall. It was barely large enough to admit a full-grown Ranthrr. Krral did something to the lock and the door sighed open. With a quick look to make sure no one was watching, Krral went rapidly down the steps the open door revealed. "It's a little tight in here," he muttered, "but the trip is a short one." Reaching the bottom of the steps, he got down on his hands and knees and began to crawl along a very cramped tunnel, filled with pipes and cables. After moving perhaps fifty feet in that manner, he came to a hatch fitted in the ceiling of the tunnel. He stopped, listened for several moments, then carefully opened the hatch and crawled out into the pitch-dark storage pantry of his own residence.

Krral crept to the door of the pantry and opened it a crack. The room beyond it, which was the front room of the habitation, was dark and still. He stood, slowly sweeping the area with piercing eyes, straining to see the slightest thing out of order.

There were two of them. Slightly darker darknesses. One to the left of the front entrance. The other on the other side of the front room next to the door to the sleeping room. Krral studied them. Although he couldn't be positive, he was convinced they both were carrying weapons. Possibly burners, the compact laser pistols the Service sometimes used in circumstances of the gravest danger.

*Score one for the Questioner,* Krral said. *You were right. Two of them. Armed.* Moving very gently, he opened one of the pouches on his harness. From it he took two long, pointed, metal spikes. *But then,* he commented wryly, *so am I. Ready?*

With a sudden, fluid movement, Krral threw open the door and stepped into the room. As he moved, he flung one of the spikes at the dark spot by the door. No sooner was the spike in the air than he was too, diving and rolling. The hiss of the burner was only inches behind him.

He came up and threw himself to the left, at the same instant flinging the second of his spikes. The burner hissed again and then Seeker heard something gasp, followed by the clunk of an object falling to the floor.

Krral was across the space between him and the second figure in an instant. He struck it once in the head, claws fully out. Gore and fur spattered out in a shower behind his stroke. The body fell heavily.

Without pausing, Krral hit the floor in another roll, moving in the direction of the front door. The figure there was still and slumped against the wall. But the burner was still in its hand. Krral sent the weapon flying in one direction, the body in the other.

He crouched, all senses alert, scouting the dark room for signs of any more enemies. The night was still as death. Slowly Krral reached up and hit the light pad.

The sudden glare showed two Ranthrr. The one nearest to them had a spike sticking directly out of its forehead. The other had a spike sticking in its throat and the lower half of the right side of its face was missing. Krral went from one to the other, staring down at them for long, silent moments. ''I know these two, Questioner,'' he finally declared flatly. ''They worked for the Service.''

He paused, his eyes leaving the bodies of the intruders and moving up to gaze into empty air. "I know who murdered, Mraal, Questioner. I know."

He sat waiting anxiously for the call that would say it was all over, that things were safe at last. Damn that Krral, he thought, if only he'd left well enough alone. But just like his nosy mate, Mraal, he hadn't been satisfied with the obvious. Maybe it had been the Questioners they both carried. Maybe that is what had made them different from the other operatives. Or maybe they were just different to begin with. Maybe all that nonsense about ancient hunting Ranth blood actually had some validity.

He stood and began to pace back and forth. Two, two sent to do the job. Trained, every bit as good as Krral. At first he'd thought poison or a bomb would be best. But he'd rejected that. Easier for him to commit suicide. One more of the mysterious deaths. Nothing even worth investigating.

A slight noise stopped him in midstride. What was that? He strained to hear more. Nothing. Just a creak. A night noise. Nothing. He heaved a sigh of relief. Nothing.

He turned to renew his pacing and stopped dead in his tracks. There was someone standing there, just in the shadows by the door to the sleeping room where he couldn't make the face out clearly. "Who . . ." he began to ask. But he knew. And his heart froze within him.

Krral stepped into the full light. "Good evening. I have to inform you that your errand boys failed miserably at their task."

"What . . . I don't know what you're talking about. What are you doing here? What are you . . ."

Krral held up one hand, his claws fully extended. The other Ranthrr shrank back. "We both know why I'm here. I'm here to complete my Blood Right. I'm here to revenge the death of Mraal. Oh, I know you didn't kill her directly yourself. But you were the one who gave the orders."

The other Ranthrr snarled and stepped back into a defensive posture, his own claws flashing out. "Damn you! Take one step and I'll summon help. I have a button right here and . . ."

Krral laughed softly. "So dramatic! Have you already forgotten that I am also an operative? I know the tricks, the defenses. The system is suffering a malfunction right now. The button will summon no one." His voice became very soft and intimate. "It's just me and you. No one will interfere."

"By all the ice on Vynnur! You won't get away with this! I'll . . ."

Krral advanced suddenly and the other Ranthrr retreated in sudden fear. He knew he was no match for a master of Dreadclaw. Krral stopped and stared at him. "Why? Why did you kill Mraal?"

The other was panting. "Because she came too close. She realized what was going on. I had to stop her."

"But why the Questioner? Why was it Called?"

"My case had to be total, unassailable. The presence of a Questioner made sure of that. No one would doubt the word of a Questioner. But when the two of them started to get too close to the truth, I had to get rid of both of them. The damn Questioner realized what was happening before Mraal did. It was smart and tough, a real warrior type. But I was ready for it. I'd already sent a party up to the ship and when it transferred back, they grabbed it. It put up an incredible fight, but they killed it. Then they dumped the body in the escape module of their own ship and blew up the Questioner's ship with a torpedo."

"Service work, wasn't it? I thought so. Only the Service has those kind of facilities. And you figured the blame would fall on Vururrl and the Righthand Pathway."

"They were the ones I was really after! I had to destroy them! They're a terrible threat to all Ranth! Surely you can see that, Krral. Vururrl is insane, a madman. His idiocy could cause incredible harm, could undermine the stability of Ranth civilization. He must be stopped. Join me, Krral. Help save our race and destroy Vururrl!"

Krral shook his head sadly. "That's not why you want to destroy Vururrl and you know it. You're sick. You've been nursing your hatred ever since Vynnur. Hiding it, oh yes, but letting it grow and fester. And now it's burst open and spread its filthy poison over the lives of others. Vururrl isn't the crazy one. You are."

"He must die! And so must all those who support him! I'll destroy them all! Help me, Krral! They killed Mraal, I swear it! It was their fault! I had no choice, I . . ."

Krral advanced slowly again. "Save your breath. You only

have a few left. I'm going to kill you. Blood Right.''

The other Ranthrr fell to his knees, his hands held out in supplication. "Questioner!" he shrieked. "If you're still there, don't let him do this! It's your duty! Save me!"

"I'm still here," Seeker said calmly. "But I'm leaving. What Krral does now is no concern of mine. I have no duty toward you, only toward providing an answer to the question I was asked. I've done that. My job is over and I'm going back to Labyrinth. Goodbye, Krral."

"Goodbye, Questioner. I know what I must do. First this. And then what we talked of. Goodbye. And thank you." There was a slight twist and he felt a sudden emptiness in his mind. Krral knew it would be there as long as he lived. It made him sad, but he knew there was nothing that could be done about it. One more thing that nothing could be done about. He shrugged and moved once more toward the kneeling Ranthrr.

"Come, Shrryl," he growled. "It's time to die."

# EPILOGUE

*Everything that has been said up to now
merely defines a way of thinking.
But the point is to live.*
        *Albert Camus*
        The Myth of Sisyphus

"I know who murdered Mraal, Questioner. I know."

"Yes," Seeker responded, "I, too, think I know. Do you know why?"

Krral shrugged. "I don't really care. Blood Right doesn't need to understand motives. It merely expiates the fact of the crime, not its reasons. Shrryl is guilty, so Shrryl must pay."

"I think I know why as well, but I'd still like to hear it from Shrryl's own mouth. I realize you're determined to kill him, but would you mind asking a few questions first? Just to satisfy my curiosity and to see if I've guessed correctly."

"No problem. I want to go now and do it." He paused. "And you? You'll be going once you have your answers?"

"Yes. Except for that, there's nothing for me to do here any longer. I'll return to Labyrinth. And what will you do, Krral? I've sensed a growing uneasiness in your mind as this case has progressed. The words of Master Grrul, Damurrl, and Vururrl seem to have made an impact on you."

Krral considered. "Impact? Yes, I suppose so. Master Grrul was a strangely compelling Ranthrr. But also strangely weak. Something about his belief in transcendence of the Paradox bothers me. I'm not sure it isn't just another version of the Ranth belief that immortality is just around the next bend in the trail. Hope is hope, and one form is no more real than another.'' He paused thoughtfully. ''Though I suppose that if Grrul dies believing he has transcended the Paradox, then in a way he has. But Grrul's path is not mine. That kind of running from trouble just isn't in my nature.

''I found Damurrl's melancholy over his unknown king to be a bit silly and affected. After all, Questioner, none of the Ranth who built that temple for that king are remembered. They died and left no individual trace behind. Why is it so much more awful that the same happened to their king? And what conceivable difference can it make, now that they are all dead? Did that king die believing in his own immortality? If so, what more is there?

''Vururrl's answer is the least satisfactory to me. Life may be a paradox, all our efforts may be futile in the face of death, but that still doesn't mean that we give them any more significance or meaning by committing suicide. Oh, I guess if I was in horrible pain, suicide might seem attractive. Just get it over with, you know. But the very fact that can feel pain also means I can feel joy. And who knows what will follow from what? And what difference does it make anyway? Deciding that suicide is a way to resolve the Paradox seems to me like deciding that one of the rules in a game is to call it off when it isn't going your way. No, I can't follow the path of Vururrl either.

''It just seems to me that both pathways try to step around the Paradox. But they end up basically in the same place, and that place is still well short of resolving the Paradox. In fact, I can't help but feel they just reconfirm it.''

''But what is left, then?'' Seeker asked softly.

Krral frowned. ''If you really carry the logic of the Paradox to its end, if you accept it and don't try to cheat or step aside or close your eyes, there's only one thing that makes any sense at all. You simply have to live with it. Or maybe I should say live *in* it. You sort of have to keep hope and despair balanced, to walk a narrow track between them. If you step off the track in either direction, you lose the way.''

''Is hope an illusion, then?''

''An illusion? No. Or at least not unless it is absolute hope. Hoping that you'll find the murderer of your mate and be able to take your Blood Right is not illusion. But hoping that doing so will somehow solve everything, well, that's illusion.

"And despair is just useless, especially as a principle to live your life by. Or to plan your death by.

"The point, Questioner, is to live your life, to do your job as it should be done. To endure. And not for any reason beyond the living itself." He paused reflectively. "It . . . isn't easy at times. I remember how I felt when my first mate was slaughtered before my eyes by that Brranth. While I was recovering in the medical center, I knew some pretty black moments. Everything seemed so futile. Love and struggle, everything seemed useless.

"But now I know that the problem was that like all other Ranth, I was measuring my loss against the infinite promise of the immortality that our science was just about to discover. I guess you just can't measure living against absolutes. Living is living. It's limited, partial, imperfect and often painful. But surely it is every bit as significant as dying."

Krral shrugged. "So I guess what I'll do after I kill Shrryl is live. And just see where it leads."

"And that was our last real conversation," Seeker finished. Longarm pulled at its lower lip with long fingers. It looked unusually thoughtful. "Ummmm, ummmmmm," the teacher mused. "This Krral interests me. I wouldn't be the least bit surprised to find him on the landing pad one of these days.

"Well, well, whatever, whatever. And so now you're back, eh? Another successful trip, eh? And ready to go zipping out on another one as soon as possible?" Longarm laughed and slapped its thigh with its hand. "But first a question, eh?"

Seeker smiled slightly. "Yes. A question, as always. After all, I am a Questioner."

"Well, to save you the trouble, Bilrog is doing well. Or as well as can be expected. Would you like to see your fine Furmorian friend?" Without waiting for an answer, Longarm turned and began to walk away from the center of Start, out toward the deadly surface of the planet.

Seeker followed the Teacher for some time. Eventually they came to a group of rocks on a hilltop. Moving warily among the rocks, they came to an open place in their center. In the middle of the open space was what looked to Seeker like a large crystal lying on its side with an impurity at its center.

At a gesture from Longarm, the ursoid approached the crystal until it was standing directly over the transparent surface. Gazing down into its depths, Seeker could make out a familiar shape. Seeker looked up at Longarm, dismay on its face. "What . . . what is this thing? Is that Bilrog in there? What's the Furmorian doing in a crystal?"

Longarm hooted. "Ha! Questions, questions, questions! But why ask me? Ask Bilrog."

*Hello, Seeker,* said a voice that spoke in the ursoid's mind.

"Bilrog? Is that you?"

*More or less,* Bilrog replied. *A lot of me is missing right now. But it's on its way back.*

Seeker shook its head. "I don't understand this. What is this crystal? Some kind of regenerating device?"

Longarm shrugged. "I don't understand it either. All I know is that I was told by Labyrinth to bring Bilrog here and leave it. I did. This crystal grew up around our friend and whatever is happening is happening."

"Bilrog, are you all right?" the ursoid asked urgently.

*I'm getting all right,* came the reply. *But I've still got a long way to go. In time, in time.*

"How long?"

There was a pause, then a slight chuckle. *I fear I don't have the answer to that. I'm dealing directly with Labyrinth, Seeker, and planets have a very different time sense than either you or I. It says, 'Soon, soon' but I have the feeling it means 'soon' in the geological sense.* There was a pause. *But I tire so easily. I must stop now. Come and see me again. Goodbye.*

As they walked back toward Start, Longarm said gently, "And H*mb*l still dances, Seeker. You can search for the hummer once you've rested."

Seeker was silent for a long time. Finally, just as they approached the buildings of Start, the ursoid gestured vaguely at Start, at the planet, and at the universe around it and asked quietly, "Why, Longarm. Why?"

The Teacher just smiled.